"The combined effect of the different styles on display here is virtuosic, but Olsen never loses sight of the bigger scope of history—or the tragedies the future will hold for most of these characters. This novel manages the impressive task of being both experimental and accessible—and thoroughly moving to boot."

—*Kirkus Reviews*

"Sparked by the exuberant energy of his own multivalent perception, ignited by the brilliance of his wildly playful imagination and unfathomably expansive compassion, Lance Olsen has translated *My Red Heaven*, Otto Freundlich's abstract cubist painting, into a novel full of dissonant shocks and thrilling confusions, a library of loss revealing the perilous ecstasies of life in Berlin between the wars. Layer by layer, he unpeels a palimpsest of paint, turning his fiercely attentive, unbounded love to every being in every moment, exposing infinite unknown dimensions, delivering us to exhilaration and terror as we watch the future and the past irradiate our present moment."

—Melanie Rae Thon, author of
The Voice of the River and *Silence and Song*

"Where to stand in this original novel as History that unspeakably painfully hurts while montaging all our astonishing, poignant, and gross ironies. Between lives, even our own, that are less here than nearby or elsewhere; between Dietrich and Heisenberg; between, on one hand (literally), Arendt and Heidegger showering and thinking about thinking, and deaths there perhaps are no words for; between what is actually, terribly being evoked and, dissolve after dissolve, an exquisite narrative prose risking again and again an incorrigible lightness. At random, I thought of Wittgenstein in Duffy's *The World as I Found It*; dictatorship in Spufford's *Red Plenty*; the sculptural work of Joseph Beuys; and, where fact seems all the more fact in a context of fictive documentation, the great Sebald."

—Jos⟨...⟩   ⟨...⟩annonball

my red heaven

lance olsen

Also by Lance Olsen

NOVELS
Live from Earth
Tonguing the Zeitgeist
Burnt
Time Famine
Freaknest
Girl Imagined by Chance
10:01
Nietzsche's Kisses
Anxious Pleasures
Head in Flames
Calendar of Regrets
Theories of Forgetting
There's No Place Like Time
Dreamlives of Debris

SHORT STORIES
My Dates with Franz
Scherzi, I Believe
Sewing Shut My Eyes
Hideous Beauties
How to Unfeel the Dead

NONFICTION
Ellipse of Uncertainty
Circus of the Mind in Motion
William Gibson
Lolita: A Janus Text
Rebel Yell: A Short Guide to Writing Fiction
Architectures of Possibility: After Innovative Writing
[[there.]]

MY RED HEAVEN

a novel by **LANCE OLSEN**

5220 Dexter Ann Arbor Rd.

Ann Arbor, MI 48103

www.dzancbooks.org

First US edition: January 2020
Interior and jacket design by Matthew Revert

Printed in the United States of America

10   9   8   7   6   5   4   3   2   1

für Andi,
und für den Koffer,
den wir immer noch dort haben

acknowledgments

The author wishes to thank the publishers of *Ascent, Autre Magazine, The Collagist, Conjunctions, Diagram, Hairstreak Butterfly Review, Heavy Feather Review, Hotel Amerika, Golden Handcuffs Review, Notre Dame Review, Numéro Cinq, South Carolina Review, Statorec, Vol. 1 Brooklyn, Weber,* and *Witness,* in which excerpts from this novel first appeared in a slightly different form; the D.A.A.D. Artists-in-Berlin Program and its fellows for their generosity and thoughtful support during his stay there in 2015 and 2016; the University Research Committee & Creative Grant and International Travel & Research Grant from the University of Utah for enabling him to further his work in Berlin; Momentum Worldwide Gallery for the residency it made possible in Berlin in the spring of 2018; and for the photographs of Berlin's lost places—Michael Kroetch: [[a radiant system]], [[bounding for birds]], [[twenty-seven seconds ago]], [[a chair is a very difficult object]], [[a hundred different movies]], [[the noise knowledge makes]], [[mother eating her own uterus]], [[we have come loose from ourselves]]; Andi Olsen: [[skin waving goodbye]], [[the heat of our thoughts]].

Somewhere, someone still remembers. Somewhere else, someone forgets.
      —Ellen Hinsey, "Eastern Apocrypha"

The forest provides the wood for the axe that will chop it down.
      —Jenny Erpenbeck, *The End of Days*

May you be born in a house on fire.
      —Attila József, "The Seventh"

underpainting

berlin : skin waving goodbye

Every evening the dead gather on rooftops across the city. Bodies, sexes, injuries, illnesses shed, they become aware over and over again that their lives are going on somewhere else without them.

Maybe they imagine others taking up where they left off, Anita Berber thinks, heroin heat seeping up her arm. She sprawls across Otto Dix's bed. Vinegar fills her mouth. Love happens. She extracts the syringe and the thought lands within her that everything wasn't all right and now everything is because her bobbed hair is red tonight, her thin heart-shaped lips.

Next year Anita will collapse on a stage in Damascus during her cabaret tour of the Middle East. Four months later she will succumb to consumption in a Kreuzberg hospital. On a November afternoon feathering with snow, she will be lowered into a pauper's grave in Neukölln. The only people present will be two cross-dressers, three ex-husbands, her lesbian lover Susi, a hooker named Hilda, and Otto Dix himself.

But all Anita knows at present is it is sometime past midnight. It is June 10, 1927. It is her twenty-eighth birthday, and earlier this evening a skinny mean cop mistook her in her tuxedo and bowtie for a man.

Her slackening awareness attempts performing an idea. Maybe that's what they do, the gathering dead, standing on those rooftops, faces raised to the flaming ocean of desire above: watch their lives going on without them. A stubby woman surprised last summer by influenza hears her silver brush (she can smell the horsehair bristles after a lavender bath) huff through a stranger's hair. A gaunt widow, whose hope gave out last month barging up the third flight of stairs to her fourth-floor flat, pictures her husband encountering the shock of a young woman's jasmine and lily perfume at the nape of her neck.

Everything wasn't all right and now everything is.

Anita is sure everything will succeed.

She can feel it in her—

Anita got so high last night she turned up half an hour late to her own dance number at The White Mouse. In the middle of her solo, she tripped over herself. Several assholes started laughing. She took a swig from the brandy bottle on a table up front and spat it over them, smug fuckers.

Only that isn't now.

Now is simply this soft heat breathing through her. Now is this overwhelming love. Anita loves that love, how she can sense everydayness leaving her, watch herself drifting into her special silver light.

She sees the world as if it is not within her, but beside her. Below her. Not within her, but across the room.

Her body sheds away from her like the bodies of the dead.

She lingers above her not-her in Otto's cluttered studio.

Linseed oil. Mildew. Late spring leafiness.

She studies how the skin people call Anita Berber allows the skin people call Otto Dix to position her limbs whichever way he wants across his narrow disarranged bed because—because he has paid her to become his little marionette—because—

Just a minute.

Just a minute.

—because Anita adores cocaine. Because after the second line she always knows she will live forever.

Her favorite drugs are chloroform and ether stirred in a porcelain bowl, whisked with a white rose, the petals of which she nibbles at elegantly like lotus flowers. The twilight sleep she drowns in is a miracle followed by another miracle followed by another.

Except Otto couldn't score any today.

Heroin is fine.

Heroin will have to do.

And so the skin people call Anita Berber allows the skin called Otto Dix to position her limbs whichever way he wants because his strong face, his slicked-back blond hair.

Because he earned the Iron Cross on the Western Front, was wounded in the neck and almost bled out. Otto says he can't remember hearing the grenade explode. He was squatting in a trench in a fog at dawn and then waking up in a hospital tent, his panicked swallowing an incongruity.

Sometimes Otto tells Anita the dream that won't leave him alone. He is crawling through narrow passage after narrow passage in a bombed-out house that has proliferated to become the universe. An incinerated corpse with shattered jaw attempts whispering something in his ear as he drags himself over it.

In place of words, a handful of thin gold necklaces and rotten teeth pour out of its mouth.

Otto painted Anita for the first time two years ago. Oil and tempera on plywood. One hundred twenty centimeters by sixty-five. He made everything in her portrait a great upsurge of red save her charcoaled eyes and penciled black brows and pale angular face and pale long-nailed hands.

The canvas felt like lust and amphetamines.

Anita couldn't stop contemplating how Otto saw her. It proved if you gave her fifteen minutes she could seduce any man or woman on the planet.

Only that isn't now.

Now is Otto working on another piece in his murdered-women series. Anita can't understand why. It's not that the idea bothers her. The problem is everyone is doing murdered women these days. George Grosz. Karl Hofer. Even Murnau in his movie with Max Schreck in frock coat, pointy ears, bad incisors, broody shadows.

What Anita wants to know is why anyone would want to do what everyone else is doing.

It takes effort to make yourself yourself.

She adores Otto, absolutely she does, but he's almost forty, for God's sake. Old men should know better.

Old men should know the secret is that if you need to act in films with titles like *The Skull of Pharaoh's Daughter*, you act in films with titles like *The Skull of Pharaoh's Daughter*. The secret is that if you need to dance nude at nineteen, show up to parties draped only in a borrowed mink with a pet monkey hanging around your neck, participate in the odd private blue movie, you reach for your zipper.

You become your own little marionette while pretending to be someone else's.

Why do you insist on painting this shit? Anita hears herself asking.

Her voice surprises her. It's slurry, nearer than she would have guessed. She thought until this second she didn't have anything to say. She had been focusing instead from a great distance on Otto's generous touch, how he is tenderly arraying the upper half of her torso over the meticulously disarranged bed's edge so the top of her head barely grazes the wide wooden floor planks.

Anita takes slow pleasure in the way his studio flips in front of her. Down is up. Up is sideways. The emerald tile stove tophats on the ceiling.

Such shit? asks Otto.

He is on his knees, arranging props around her.

Ugly dead women, darling, Anita says. Everybody's doing them. Would you like a bit of advice?

Otto stops adjusting a fallen desk chair.

You need to paint me more often. Everybody knows how gorgeous I am. It would do wonders for your bank account.

Otto chuckles. Anita imagines the double row of bushy trees running up the middle of the cobblestone street outside the window. The brown-sugar sand running up between them. How in this city you have the impression bits of countryside are always only steps away.

Don't forget, Otto says. I also paint ugly dead men.

Anita parts her thin red lips because she has something to add, a comeback, a quip, only she forgets what it is because—

—because the myriad leaves, thousands and thousands of them on this street alone, the dewy green scent tinged with coal fumes.

Anita senses her concentration smearing into the yellow blur you see when you stand on an U-Bahn platform and refuse to blink as the cars rush past.

You're missing, Anita says. My point. Do you happen—

The rest of her sentence misplaces itself.

And they're not ugly at all, Otto responds. They're beautiful. Just like you.

—happen to have a pillow, darling? I'd like to catch a catnap while you genius along.

Everything's beautiful, he says, handing her a red satin cushion from the bed somewhere up by her heels. Geraniums. Barbed wire. Gas masks. Radio waves. Those endless runways at Tempelhof. They're beautiful because they're the world. By definition, they can't be anything else.

Anita doesn't care.

She tries to care, but it's just not in her.

All she can do is love the dead staring up from those rooftops. They're bodiless, only somehow she can still make out their mouths, atmospheric vibrations that used to be something else, opening in astonishment, one by one, at the immense flaming ocean churning in the sky.

The way they lift their right arms, perhaps pointing, perhaps waving goodbye.

The way, as she looks on, the gesture resolves into a salute.

17

loss library : shrapnel

Otto sits cross-legged before Anita, studying the contours of her face. Shoes off. Sleeves rolled up on the pale green surgical gown he likes to wear while painting. He touches a palm to her hair and startles at its stiffness.

At the end of the block a streetcar clanks by.

Upstairs his neighbor, the crouping ferret with cockeyed jaw, clumps through his flat, out the front door, down to the water closet on the half-landing.

Hinges squeak open.

Hinges squeak shut.

Otto becomes aware of himself dissolving into the hours that are no longer about language.

Anita was frantically reckless only a couple years ago with her immaculate skin and dark eyes and acerbic curiosity. She arrived in Berlin ready to eat life. She wanted to show up everywhere, meet everyone, sample every powder or fluid or pill anyone offered her.

Now she is this chalky makeup.

This loss library.

She was already looking a little sharp-cornered when Otto first met her. Sickly thin. A decade and a half older than she was.

Her heart had already become a rain of tiny dead yellow flowers.

Before that—Otto rises, rubbing the back of his neck, satisfied Anita has left herself for a while—before that she was this stunning sixteen-year-old raised by her grandmother in Dresden.

Over the years, she became a different kind of beauty: more significant, convincing, lasting—as if her interior had slowly emerged and spread across her exterior.

She turned out to be the saddest person Otto has ever met.

You can catch darkness from her, if you're not careful. Otto loves her so hard for that, loves her most thoroughly where she is most ruined.

He takes his place behind his easel. Raises his fine-pointed paintbrush. Pecks a glob of glossy crimson on the palette.

Hesitates.

Feels less like a particular human being than a confusion of occasions.

Otto lowers his paintbrush, watching Anita step off the train from Dresden into the madhouse of the city's main station, secondhand suitcase by her side. The great vaulted roof. The lightflood from the great vaulted windows. Onions, sauerkraut, coal smoke, wet steel, fresh pretzels, sweat.

He watches himself squatting in a trench. Fog had settled thick across the wintry earth pocked with mortar craters, braided with barbed wire, littered with abandoned helmets, rifles, legs like old wet branches. Otto could barely make out the soldiers squatting on either side of him. The lack of sleep left him jittery and out of focus. He rose carefully, trying to situate himself, and then he was waking up in a hospital tent, bite of chlorine disinfectant burning his sinuses, unable to turn his head or swallow, struggling against two nurses' imperatives.

When he began getting to his feet that morning, boots sloshing icy mud, Otto Dix believed enthusiastically in the cause. He had left his father in an iron foundry, his seamstress mother in the kitchen, and enlisted in the army to help make his country's destiny happen. First he fought in a field artillery regiment down south, then in a machine gun unit on the Western Front.

Yet as his body crumpled out from under him, Otto came to understand you either leave a trench like that believing in some invisible sky daddy with a bushy white blessedness, or you leave it believing in exactly nothing at all.

Otto struggled against those two nurses, his only goal to bring into being reminders for the world that to be alive is to be beaten, broken, demolished, and to be beaten, broken, demolished is to embody the purest form of beauty.

He picks up the fine-pointed brush again, considers the small wood panel he will cover with Anita, commences applying tempera underpainting. He will follow this with a thin glaze in the manner of the old masters. The coolness of Holbein. The delirious precision of Bosch.

A new holiness, which has come so close to truth that the Wallraf-Richartz Museum in Cologne chose to hide one of his reminders behind a curtain when it was exhibited. Step through, and you entered a blasted landscape with a blackened corpse in shredded uniform hanging from a burnt tree's limb. The mayor forced the museum's director to resign for his curatorial indiscretion.

Anita isn't a person. Anita is a country. She is Germany splayed upside down, legs spread, knees raised, draping off a narrow bed, arms hanging limp by her limply hanging head, knife still jutting out from between her legs, blood soaking the groin of her nightshift, her mutilated stomach, pooling out from under her stiff dry hair.

Behind her, to the right: a window through which will appear in the finished version, not Otto's treed street, but another, shrilly empty one, except for a row of orderly four-story buildings receding into tedium.

That symmetry will be undone by the sacred mess inside.

The scene's orientation will make viewer into murderer.

When Otto glances up again he finds early morning sunlight frosting his studio. He wants to say he is in the capital, only he can't be sure. He wants to say it is just past 4:30, yet that's just a guess.

How did time stop being time?

He doesn't recollect lifting Anita into bed, tucking her beneath the quilt, plumping her pillow for her.

Still, there she is on her back, modestly snoring.

She will continue snoring modestly for another thirty, forty minutes before waking confused and afraid. Otto will sit on the edge of the bed and try to comfort her. It won't work. What she will need isn't comfort. What she will need is another hit. And what she will do is demand one, half little-girl whine, half dominatrix diktat. Only Otto won't have another hit to give.

Anita has to leave herself for a while every day. Otto accepts that. But she has to return to herself eventually, too.

Another thirty, forty minutes, and Otto will help her dress.

Another thirty, forty minutes, and he will help prepare her for what comes next, lend her whatever spare cash he has lying around, usher her, dazed and doddering, out the front door, down the stairwell, into the vicious sunshine.

Otto will try to catch a few hours' sleep himself before the bombed-out houses whirl in. When he wakes he will wash, dress in the same clothes he wears now, and take the long stroll over to Potsdamer Platz's star-shaped intersection, where he will sketch on Café Josty's leafy veranda, caught up in engine noise, people noise, bowler hats and shrinking dresses, the traffic light tower, how a metropolis moves.

Sketching across from the Grand Hotel Esplanade allows him to concentrate even when he can't concentrate.

Once he saw Charlie Chaplin coming down the hotel's steps. There was no mistaking it. Nobody noticed him because he wasn't trying to be noticed. Chaplin had figured out how to look like anyone else when he wanted. He walked down the steps like he was just another guy and gave himself over to the crowd flowing around him.

The Tramp was there.

The Tramp was gone.

Otto found that moment's ordinariness stunning.

This evening George Grosz will host a modest dinner party with a few friends—Max Herrmann-Neisse among them, that beaky bald hunchbacked poet and critic always looking a little like the luxurious chair he is sitting in is trying to ingest him. Then Otto will stroll home to sink back into his work, unaware that within a dozen years inoffensive landscapes will be the only subject matter the new regime will allow him to paint—the odd village, the mildly reverent rainbow—while learning how much can be taken away from a person, even his own nightmares.

Now, however, he is watching the day come into being. He pictures how all across the city whores are melting away into millinery shops, cafés, tenements. How produce trucks are rolling into market squares and offloading barges along the canals.

He unlatches the window, swings it open to let in a chilly gust, hears a horse-drawn delivery van jangling up the street, takes in a man and woman walking their dog below, a lean Doberman with cropped ears and docked tail.

At the Tempelhof airfield people are already queuing for flights to Paris, Zurich, Moscow.

In bars the owners are mopping the floors.

This will be his city for another little while, then it will gradually bridge to others.

The couple below pauses beneath a linden to share a cigarette.

Their Doberman squats daintily on the brown-sugar sand beside the path and pees imperiously.

bounding for birds : mathematics

The Doberman's name is Delia. Delia won't see the end of this day. She doesn't know that. What she knows is she's on the longest, most glorious walk of her life. There is no time but this time, no place but this place. She can scarcely endure all the smells and sounds and touches and tastes inside her. She is with her masters and they have given her these radiant gifts and it is impossible to conceive of a way to thank them enough.

She doesn't understand the name of the woman behind her is Elise Lemme. She doesn't understand the man's name is Otto Hampel.

Otto and Elise woke Delia improbably early this morning, asking her if she wanted to go out. Delia always wants to go out. That is her only knowledge. The flat she lives in is too small, the air in it too used up, presence nowhere except on the other side of the front door.

The whole of Delia's day, the whole of Delia's life, is an almost unendurable waiting for two questions: *Do you want to go out, girl? Is that what you want?*

She bounds from her dream (in which she is bounding for birds on the grassy shores of the Schlachtensee) and, barking rapturously, bounds from her masters' bed toward her bowl beside the stove. She wolfs down her food, feels the choker collar going on, the leash clicking into place. Somewhere behind her she senses her tail nub, over which she is continuously bewildered she possesses no will, furiously aspiring to wag.

And now she is here.

And now she is here.

And now she is here.

Delia has no room for any other idea in her head.

Elise is making several short loudnesses in the direction of Otto. Delia can't grasp what they mean. Delia doesn't care. All she cares about is this flawless motion she is inhabiting. All she cares about is the prosperity of aromas and music through which she advances. How can one being celebrate them all? Morning soil. Clang gods. Urine echoes. Flower breaths. The indescribably compelling shits of other dogs—some shoe polishers no taller than Delia's hocks, some small-bear huge and hairy, some agile, some nervous, some crippled, some cocky, some bereft, some almost as elated as Delia herself.

Delia savors the elementary pleasure that she could kill them all.

Elise says to Otto, smoke bulging from her mouth up into the acute morning nip: I feel like an idiot.

It's not going to rain today, Otto says. He considers the enlivening sky through the branches, adds: It should rain on a day like this.

Maybe we should give it more thought, says Elise.

She is twenty-three, barely finished grammar school before dropping away from ruler smacks to become a domestic servant, and now her hands look forty-five, puffy, reddish, big-knuckled. Otto is twenty-seven, large-eared, thin-lipped, meager-chinned. He fell into factory work after the war and cherishes Elise's hands because they tell him the same story every time he looks at them: I know what it feels like. *I know how to pilot this place.*

Maybe we haven't done the math right, Elise says.

But she already knows there's no more math left to do. The numbers are the numbers. If there were more numbers to do, they would do them.

Otto opens his mouth to respond. Elise's frown stills him. Wordless, they finish the cigarette they're splitting. Otto kneels, calls over Delia, clicks off her leash. The Doberman wavers, wavers, looking up at him for guidance. Otto pulls a fist-sized dirty white ball from the pocket of his double-breasted coat and rises and chucks the ball far down the path between the lindens.

Delia blasts after it, passing a funny-eyed old woman with long gray hair, who drags her large leather purse on the ground behind her like a dead poodle.

Otto lights another cigarette, sucks the smoke deep into the abundant branches of his lungs, passes it to Elise, trying to let the sear in his chest overrun him. Near the end of the path Delia scoops up the ball, brakes two meters farther on, spins, and, imagining the skull of a small animal between her jaws—a squirrel, a baby—blasts back toward them, an ecstatic black visual slur.

Sentence fragments orbit Otto's head. He decides not to speak any of them. Instead he kneels again, calls Delia over, clicks her leash back on. Elise bends and fluffles the dog's neck and face and ears.

And now Delia is here.

And now she is here.

And now she is here.

And now, slobbery dirty white ball in her mouth, she is trotting someplace else. She can't wait to discover where. She pushes forward into sunlight, proud, whirring with joy, oblivious that at the end of this walk she will meet a long line of puzzled fellow dogs. Delia will wait alertly with them, fragrances and loudnesses boisterous around her, confident her masters have the situation in hand, and at the end of that line a sour-smelling man in a white lab coat will unceremoniously yank her choker tight as if she had just misbehaved (although she will be sure she hasn't) and shove her into an airtight metal box with three other baffled yipping dogs whom Delia has never met (at which point her tail stub will stop wagging), slam down the door, and flip on the gas valve.

For just under a minute Delia will remember bounding at those birds in her dream, feeling as if she is at the gray edge of waking again, and then she will be over.

By the time the sour-smelling man in the white lab coat opens the door, Otto and Elise will be gone, already several blocks closer to their flat in gritty Wedding, wordless, just two other dog owners among thousands who couldn't pay the raised canine tax.

They will miss Delia desperately for months, alternating between unconditional numbness and so much anxiety they will feel everything will go on fire in ten seconds. They will relive that last betrayal—that line of rattled dogs, that metal box, that look in Delia's eyes as the vet bent toward her—sometimes together, sometimes alone, and then less and less, because, they will learn, that's how damage diminishes itself in the human body.

Eight years, and they will wake up married.

Five more, and Elise will open her front door to be handed a telegram informing her that her brother has been killed in action somewhere in France fighting for something she can no longer fathom.

In the thirty seconds it will take her to read and reread that telegram, everything will become whiteness.

Perhaps as a means to honor her brother, her dog, all the feelings Elise and Otto almost forgot they were once capable of experiencing, the couple will begin writing hundreds of postcards in clumsy script and bad grammar that urge their recipients to refrain from donating money to their government, refuse military service, resist the thing their country has become.

Elise and Otto will leave those postcards in apartment block stairwells and on park benches, in mailboxes and beneath neighbors' doors.

Almost every one of them will be picked up by strangers and handed over to the Gestapo. The sheer number will lead the Gestapo to conclude they are dealing with a large, well-orchestrated, wide-ranging conspiracy.

It will take nearly eighteen months for them to realize they are wrong.

Seventeen years after he throws Delia's dirty white ball down that path for the last time, a weighted and angled guillotine blade in a backyard work shed at Plötzensee Prison will drop through Otto's neck.

The blade will be reset and three minutes later drop through Elise's.

Both Hampels will be strapped onto their backs so they can see their futures flying toward them.

What will be unusual about their executions is that nothing will be unusual about their executions. Otto's and Elise's punishments will constitute two among the nearly three thousand carried out in that work shed. Like all relatives of the beheaded and hanged in Plötzensee, theirs will be obliged to pay a fee of 1.50 Reichsmark for every day their family members spent in their cells, three hundred for the execution itself, and twelve pfennigs to cover postage for the invoice of expenses.

Like all bodies of those executed at Plötzensee, Otto's and Elise's will be released to Herr Professor Doctor Hermann Stieve, physician at the University of Berlin, who with his students will dissect them for research purposes. The results over the years will generate two hundred and thirty important academic papers, including one providing irrefutable evidence the rhythm method is not effective in preventing pregnancy.

Now, though, none of that is happening.

It is just Otto and Elise strolling along a sandy path between two rows of trees on a bluing day. Just Delia trotting proudly in front of them, leading the way toward that envelope containing the invoice of expenses.

A black shadow scrambles across their feet and flickers out.

Elise thinks *cloud*.

She reflexively raises her head to spot in the apartment block across the street two white faces hovering in two otherwise black windows, one directly above the other, peering down at her without expression.

value study

newsreel : one

Emelka Corporation

presents

—TODAY'S MOST THRILLING NEWS—

~ GERMAN CHEMIST CURES DIABETES ~

The future happens in Germany
TODAY!

Dr. Richard Meissner announces
—SPECTACULAR DEVELOPMENT—
insulin substitute *horment*!

With his lovely wife at the Berlin opera.

Cheap tablets—no injections—COMPLETE SUCCESS
in human trials!

~ NEW LUXURY LINER LAUNCHED ~

BEHOLD—*Cap Arcona* !

Our country's FINEST !
A *breathtaking* accomplishment
FOR GERMANY
206 meters long—5 decks—8 steam
turbines—2 massive propellers !

1315 PASSENGERS IN 1ST-CLASS
ACCOMMODATIONS !

~ GERMANY LOSES TRUE GIANT ~

Glaciologist Eduard Brückner dies at 64 !

Foremost expert on alpine glaciers.

With collaborator Albrecht Penck
—on the mighty Zugspitze last year—
OUR PIONEER TO THE END !

Their *Alps in the Ice Age* a standard
reference volume around the world.

Climate change
affects economy & social structure !
Brückner warned.

~ WORLD'S BIGGEST DOG ~

Here's something to BARK about !

Irish Wolfhound
—13 months—80 kilos—2.5 meters tall—

BIRTHDAY PRESENT

FOR THE YOUNGSTERS ?

~ OUR HEARTY NATION ~

Steeple chases ! Bike races ! Boxing !

It's SPORTS as usual in—

inside the storm : gray ghosts flocking

The white face hovering four meters above Otto Dix's belongs to Dora Diamant, daughter of a small businessman and rabbi in the Hasidic dynasty southeast of Warsaw. Dora is the last lover of an author whose lungs over the course of a year scarred into white clouds flocked with gray ghosts.

She is thinking about him.

She has been thinking about him all night.

Those glistery brown eyes she fell into four years ago at a holiday camp on the Baltic coast, those cheeks and chin jagged as an Expressionist woodcut, that tall nattily dressed lankiness with a decade and a half on her.

Curled among sheets, drained by all the not-remembering she had to carry out the day before, Dora spent the night staring at him spread across the back of her eyelids like a continuous detonation.

In the bluing daylight, memory becomes another thing.

In the bluing daylight, it shrinks to hurt the size of a carved jewelry box she can fit in her purse.

Dora fingers a strand of short wavy brown hair and attends the couple walking their dog below. Her head is lit less and less with Franz and her sitting on a park bench in the Tiergarten a few blocks away. They are eating ham sandwiches (their little joke) while talking about Yiddish literature and Zionism. It is sunny and April and breezy and there her lover is, dying right next to her, just like everyone right next to you is dying.

Franz told her he hated newspapers because they reminded him how unemployment had crested a quarter million here, how street fighting between extremists on the right and extremists on the left broke out nearly every day.

He preferred the foliaged peace of the park and strolls through their neighborhood to the bakery, vegetable stand, butcher's shop, where his most important decision involved selecting the right loaf of bread or pair of bratwurst links for dinner. He preferred sitting in the café overlooking Wilmersdorf Lake, sipping coffee crowned with whipped cream and describing the restaurant he wanted to open with Dora one day in Tel Aviv. It would be cozy and unassuming. Just two or three tables inside, four or five on the sidewalk beneath a dark red awning. Tidy, well-managed, situated in another orbit altogether from the one he had inhabited at the Worker's Accident Insurance Institute for the Kingdom of Bohemia for what had turned out with surprise to be his whole life.

Most of all, he preferred making fun of fathers. His, he said, was like the school bully who used to beat you up, not because he didn't like you, but because you just happened to be standing in front of him.

Dora nicknamed hers The Great Obtuseness: all cartoonish long beard, earlocks, black kaftan, fur hat, cinched mind—the bleak righteous household dispenser of shame. He wanted Dora to marry an upstanding man in the dynasty and teach in the local Orthodox religious school.

So she ran away.

She made it as far as the German border before he caught up and forced her back into the raging flavorlessness.

So she ran away again, this time to Berlin, a city where you could think what you wanted and sleep with whom you wanted and eat ham sandwiches while discussing Zionism and Yiddish literature with your dying lover on a sunny bench in the Tiergarten.

That's where they were, what they were doing, when a little blond girl stepped out of the bushes. She was crying. Franz slipped off the bench and kneeled before her, took her by the shoulders, asked gently what the matter was.

The girl told him she had lost her doll.

Franz told her not to worry. In fact, he said, he had just heard from none other than the doll herself. She wasn't lost at all. Rather, she was enjoying a lovely holiday on an island off the coast of Greece.

Everyone needs a holiday once in a while, he told the little blond girl. Work can be quite difficult. Don't you agree?

She nodded her head *yes yes yes*.

The girl's doll had even sent him a letter describing the fun she was having, Franz went on.

Suspicious, the little girl asked to see it.

Franz told her he didn't happen to have it with him at the moment, but would bring it the very next day.

When Dora and he returned home, he disappeared into their bedroom, returning half an hour later with the letter written in his odd longhand with all those plump white spaces between stubby words, giant R's and W's, thickly crossed T's and F's.

He delivered it to the little blond girl just as he had promised.

The day after that he delivered another, and the next day another, and so on for two weeks.

Soon he began worrying how he could provide the little girl with a conclusion to her story that wouldn't make her unhappier than she had been when she had first appeared.

After much thought, Franz hit upon the solution: the doll's next letter would tell about the handsome prince she had met on Santorini. It would tell about the unbelievable light and love at first sight and how the prince and the doll quickly became engaged and were already engrossed in wedding preparations. They were drawing up plans for their new home together in America, where the Statue of Liberty with his tremendous raised sword welcomes people sailing between his legs toward Ellis Island, where Manhattan skyscrapers grow right out of the wheat fields backed by the Rocky Mountains.

Once married, the doll would naturally be unable to visit her former mistress.

Is that all right? Franz asked after she had read the letter. Can you see it in your heart to understand such love?

The little blond girl pursed her lips, pondered, looked right up into his glistery brown eyes and said solemnly that she understood completely.

Watching the couple's dog—a Doberman, large and black and sinewy—rip up the path after a white ball, Dora shuts her eyes to make Franz and the little girl go away. His voice remains.

That's how all stories work, sweetheart, it says. People always live happily ever after until they don't. Every story is also always about night.

Less than a year after they met at the holiday camp on the Baltic coast, consumption closed his throat. At first she loved him but wasn't sure she liked him. Next she liked him but wasn't sure she loved him. And finally she was enraged at him for dying like this all over the place.

Dora watched him collapse into himself amid coughs, fevers, night sweats, and bloody handkerchiefs. He resembled a doll himself, a ragdoll with all the stuffing torn out, skeletal, depleted, propped among pillows in a bed at Herr Professor Doctor Hoffmann's sanatorium in Kierling near Vienna—and, nonetheless, he edited his stupid tale about that stupid artist, unnoticed and unappreciated, who himself collapsed into himself like a ragdoll with all the stuffing torn out in a pile of dirty straw in a rusting cage in the middle of a town square.

Even when Franz couldn't eat, couldn't tolerate any sort of noise whatsoever (Dora had to speak to him in whispers), could barely endure her brief touch, he could always daydream a page of juridical prose into being.

Dora was enraged at him for that, too.

Everybody thinks literature is about things that occur out there, he once told her. People believe that's what it has always been about and always will be. This is an admirable theory, but thoroughly wrong. Every age gets the literature it deserves. This one deserves a literature in which nothing takes place out there, again and again. Everything occurs in here—he pointed to his head—inside the storm.

When they first met, Dora was a twenty-six-year-old kindergarten teacher and seamstress in an orphanage. She had just changed the spelling of her last name from Dymant to Diamant to help shed her father.

She didn't know who she was and slowly she did and now (the Doberman is trotting proudly back to its owners, ball in mouth)—now she is an actress in Düsseldorf.

Just think of it.

She is staying in a friend's flat (a fellow actor working for the month in Paris), taking on the role of the sister in a short run of Jacob Gordin's *The Savage One*—the very play Franz stumbled across more than a decade ago about an idiot boy hiding in his room for fear of his brutal father. Franz wrote about it in his diaries and amplified it into a novella about a traveling salesman named Gregor Samsa.

Who could have imagined starting there and arriving here, at this window, in this flat?

The memory of a hot spring night rushes her. It had been a bad morning, a bad afternoon. Because Franz could no longer speak, he had to write down everything he wanted to say on little slips of paper.

He handed her one with two words scribbled across it: *Burn everything.*

Dora read it twice.

She looked at him wrapped in his bewilderment of quilts and smiled affectionately.

She left the room and reappeared with a matchbook, a dustbin, and the box of his writings.

Far into the unhours she helped him set fire to page after page after page.

She read the note twice and looked down at him and smiled affectionately because she knew immediately she wouldn't do what he had asked.

How could she?

That would be like setting Franz himself alight.

Dora laid a hand upon his hot cheek and did what he asked, except she held back her favorite blue octavo notebooks, the ones he had been working on the last few months, and, needless to say, the thirty-six letters he had written to her. They weren't his any longer. They belonged to Dora. Ask any lawyer. Ask any lover.

She promised herself she would see these things published one day.

Today she has too many things to live, but when she is older, when she is ready, when she is someone else, she will travel to Munich, Frankfurt, Dresden, anywhere that will have her, and share Franz Kafka with them.

A black shadow scrambles across the lindens and flickers out.

Dora thinks *cloud.*

She reflexively raises her head to spot the sun mirroring off a small metal airplane descending toward Tempelhof.

That's what hope looks like, she believes for an instant.

And then she doesn't.

chocolate : the heat of our thoughts

There is no need to compose any more poems, it strikes one of the passengers aboard that flight as he squints down at Berlin.

Forests and lakes dwindle into canals and railroad tracks fissure among factory smokestacks, warehouses, red-roofed housing blocks—the bunched commotion of Potsdamer Platz through silver haze.

There is no need to compose any more poems, because everything has already become a poem.

The passenger sets a square of chocolate-covered marzipan on his tongue to reward himself for the insight. Flinches as the sugar tinfoils his molars. This is how as much as a kilo of the stuff disappears into him every day. Chocolate tastes, he wants to say, casting for a metaphor, like love. His pushy dentist ordered him to stop, warned him sugar is the reason his gums are red and swollen, why they bleed when he brushes, why his breath smells like cat turds and those creamy abscesses break out across the inside of his cheeks.

It has reached the point where he is anxious even to enter that idiot's office, yet, after all, he is 177 centimeters tall, weighs 70 kilos. What numbers could better represent the ordinary?

Granted: his blood pressure is a bit high—yet whose isn't, given knowledge?

Granted: he produces throughout the course of a day perhaps more gas than strictly average, suffers from a growing bloat that compels him to loosen his belt buckle one notch by four every afternoon, another by bedtime.

(There are few greater pleasures than unfastening one's trousers late in the evening and feeling one's belly plump into itself again.)

Surely his vegetarianism offers a counterbalance to his well-deserved daily lapse into the paradise of cocoa, butter, vanilla, and almond paste.

And even that idiot dentist can't uncover anything amiss with a hard-working burgher taking some simple pleasure in a teaspoon of sugar dunked into a glass of red wine, can he?

Remember, all said and done, those women on the Titanic, his friend Joseph once advised him.

They waved off the dessert cart.

The single engine on the nose of the Lufthansa Junkers powers back.

His friend Joseph begins outlining the morning: There will be a car waiting. It will take us directly to our nine o'clock. All the party leaders will be there. Let us review our—

Do you know what I said to Putzi Hanfstaengl when he told me my mustache was unfashionable?

Your speech here last month was superb. Five thousand followers. There couldn't be a better way to—

I told him: If it is not the fashion now, it soon will be.

He sets another chocolate-marzipan square on his tongue, flinches, waits for his friend to join him in an appreciative chortle.

And in the reddest city outside Moscow, Joseph pushes on. *Five thousand.* All we've got to do today is build on th—

What do you think of his proposal to use *Sieg Heil* as our rallying cry? Hanfstaengl says such shit worked wonders at Harvard football games. Charges the atmosphere. Gets those feelings of togetherness going. You know: one voice, one mind.

This morning, his friend continues, we will also be speaking to a number of supporters who have—how does one say it?—have become comfortable with using their money as a bulwark against disorder.

We could repeat the phrase, say, twice. *Sieg Heil. Sieg Heil.* Like that.

We should no doubt consider—

Three times, of course, is another option.

I don't believe I would want to commit one way or another without further reflection.

The exchange between the two men becomes invisible.

The first man pokes at his sore gums with his sore tongue. The second knows the first well enough to let him return to the present in his own time.

You've done a commendable job with preparations, Joseph, the first man starts up again. You know how much I appreciate your efforts. Through them we are accomplishing something important.

I'm no more than one of many mechanisms to bring about change. The Party is the fuel. You're the heat of our thoughts.

I have a question for you.

By all means, Mein Führer.

I would ask you to take a moment to think before answering.

Of course.

Do *your* teeth hurt when you eat chocolate?

The first man's ears clog.

He opens his mouth to force a yawn.

Chin lowered, Joseph lets twenty seconds dissolve, answers: No. I can't say they do.

Interesting. I'm progressively convinced three times is far better than two. That strikes me as the rhythm of hysteria.

Perhaps we could combine that with our salute.

You *see*: politics is *precisely* like religion, only honest. He seems to have a head on his shoulders, that Hanfstaengl. For a businessman and pianist, I mean, caught up in all that Christian bilge. Do you know what else it contains?

Christianity?

Chocolate. Caffeine, a stimulant. Good for the heart and brain. A vegetarian compound, I might add. Our animal friends remain free from harm. Don't you think I'd look good before a crowd giving our salute while proclaiming our war cry?

I should mention the press will be joining us. No need to worry. We should consider them the keyboard upon which we play.

I like that. They pick the instrument. We pick the tune.

Another chocolate-covered marzipan square as the plane banks over the Spree, banks again, levels for its final descent from the east.

The first man watches the earth ease up to meet him.

Tear out Potsdamer and Anhalter railroad stations, and you have space for a three-mile-long avenue running from Tempelhof in the south to the Reichstag in the north. Two and a half times longer than the Champs-Élysées. Twenty-three meters wider. At the far end a domed assembly hall sixteen times the size of St. Peter's able to seat one hundred fifty thou—

He flinches, counts one, two, three, *Sieg Heil, Sieg Heil, Sieg Heil,* until the tinfoiling fades.

You know, Joseph, these are good times for us.

I can feel it in my blood, Mein Führer.

And thus we have a crucial duty before us: we must enjoy our enjoyment. May I take this occasion to offer a modicum of advice?

By all means.

One day you will die, Joseph. This is the sad truth of it all. And one day I shall. But on all the other days—and this is the part to keep in mind, always—on all the other days we shall not.

white silence : frozen music

Piloting through thronged Alexanderplatz, Werner Heisenberg contemplates bird nests.

Heedless of the tiny silver star descending above him, of the horns, motors, carriage wheels, creaking vegetable carts, the square's warfare of noises, he moves in a spotless white silence on his way to catch the nine thirty to Leipzig. This evening he will deliver a lecture at the university that will summarize his findings. Afterward, he will dine with several senior faculty members to finalize his new post as department head and professor of theoretical physics.

He is acutely indifferent.

Or, no, that's not quite right: he cares very much, just not about that new post. He cares about how his new post translates into leaving behind his mentor Niels Bohr at the University of Copenhagen, into returning to Germany's viscera and a sweep of unexpectedness.

Werner knows Werner thrives in such shaky, adrenalized spaces.

(Circumventing a duet of men in black fedoras basking in their own cigar smoke, dodging a soldier still in uniform, tin cup between his veed legs, bee-lining through a data-point cloud of boys in brown pants tucked into their socks playing tag among all this life, Werner is immune to the fact that in two years a virtually unknown graduate student in philosophy

44

will cross the very same stretch of Alexanderplatz, bee-lining on a slightly different trajectory, en route from Vienna to Cambridge to be examined on his thesis, a thin volume titled *Tractatus Logico-Philosophicus.* Some in the examination room will later report the more they listened to Ludwig Wittgenstein speak, the shorter they felt.)

Werner moves in a spotless white silence, contemplating bird nests while composing his lecture:

I mean by *wave packet* a wavelike disturbance whose

Wave packet signifies a wavelike disturbance whose amplitude is not the same as

By *wave packet* is meant a wavelike disturbance whose amplitude is appreciably different from zero only in a bounded regi—

He had planned to put the thing together on the overnight train. Instead he found himself tangled in a *Berliner Tageblatt* article. Amid recent restoration of the capital's cathedral, workers exposed a palimpsest of bird nests aggregated beneath the decayed roof. They had been built over several centuries. Time itself had become a solid residue. Years had turned into an avian archaeology you could touch, cup in the palm of your wonder.

Generations of jackdaws and swifts had constructed comfort by pilfering people's hair strands, yarn snags, yard trash, candy wrappers, broom bristles, wedding rings, sock scraps, fish ribs, leather gloves, peppermint gum, promissory notes, bills of sale, even tiny bits of banknotes for one thousand Russian rubles, fortunes from three thousand kilometers away.

There were snippets of orchestral compositions.

What might have been bits of diaries or encyclopedias or medical textbooks.

An architecture of frozen music.

This region is, generally, in motion, and also changes size and shape—i.e., the disturbance expands.

The velocity of the electron corresponds to that of the wave packet, but this latter cannot be exactly defined, because—

—because the recipes, the concert tickets, the packaging—it is as if all Berlin were in those nests: its sociohistorical substructures, overlays, overlaps, its pastness a splendid geological formation.

Werner imagines describing to Bohr the snarls of eighteenth-century love notes—*I wake filled with thoughts of—toxicating evening which we spent yesterday has left my—olce amor, a thousand kisses; but give none in return, for they set my—*

A transcendence of theory proved by sparrows.

Werner imagines Bohr's and his mutual enchantment, for here is tangible documentation that allows us, on the one hand, to see complex natural connections, and, on the other, to see how we can speak of them only in a batch of blundering parables.

Werner and Bohr will take delight in proof that the physicist's objective is to fall through the visible into the invisible, down, down, down, through brick walls and teacups and parquet floors into shivering atomic fog.

Just last week his mentor leaned over his hefeweizen at the bar and shouted at Werner above the babel: *You know, don't you, Heisenberg, that some subjects are so serious one can only joke about them?*

Then Bohr winked.

Werner blinked, rattled.

Swimming deeper and deeper into the conversation with himself, he somehow fails to notice someone—perhaps that attractive young woman to his left? one of the boys dodging, ducking, laughing to his right?—bump into him, beg his pardon, and vanish back into the fleshy commotion.

Late to his own accident, Werner reflects rather on how the rest of Europe can cackle all it wants about Germany buckling in the war.

The truth remains: its science is second to none.

He cuts right, through the colossal domed railway station's main doors, and only now, only as he steps into the vast echo and thrum of the huge half cylinder, commences mounting the steps toward his platform, does he startle and stop.

His back pocket, he realizes, has become infinitesimally lighter than it was three minutes ago.

(Reaching for that lack automatically, thinking *my wallet*, he is immune to the fact that in seventeen and a half years he will stand behind another podium in another mahogany-lined room, this one at a physics conference in Zurich. An American in the meager audience of professors and graduate students will finger a pistol in his pocket, weighing the pros and cons of murdering him. The American's name is Moe Berg. A mediocre catcher on the best of days, average as he will prove to be in baseball, Moe will excel in Japanese, French, Italian, Spanish, Portuguese, and German studies. During the offseason, he will complete a law degree at Columbia University and take a position at a Wall Street firm, from which the Office of Strategic Services will recruit him to attend that lecture one December evening and ascertain whether or not the physicist before him gives an indication the Germans are hatching an atomic bomb. If so, Moe has orders to shoot him. But Moe will hear nothing, and so will leave the lecture leaving history alone.)

Werner, a good-looking man in a shabby olive tweed jacket, pauses on the stairs leading up to the platform from which his train will depart.

As if working through a perplexing equation, he carefully pats himself down: first his trousers, then his jacket, next his various pockets, some real, some fancied.

Pedestrians spill around him.

A black shadow scrambles across his feet and flickers out.

Werner thinks *cloud.*

He reflexively raises his head to spot a large bird rising into the building's steel framework.

A warbler, perhaps.

Perhaps a pigeon.

tasty bitch machine : whatever sex you wish

—and Lisa and me stepping forward without trading looks into the crowds milling across Alexanderplatz shopping snacking standing sitting drinking waiting for trains trams buses taxis waiting for us without knowing that's who they're waiting for and who would have thought a sky could be such a blue and the world not end immediately maybe that preacher over there shouting in front of the fountain maybe I'll pinch one of his Bibles walk up to him tell him I'll have nicked all his money by one o'clock not a thing he can do about it him selling his daily dose of fear to passersby of shame disguised as compassion to buy the next shot of absinthe green fairy green hour lovely words leave it to the French worms in the brain gaslight striking the tarts' powdered faces around him because even the devil's grandmother was a nice girl when she was young because the pros never look like pros that's the key just me just this cute nineteen-year-old schoolteacher giving off the sex they smell perfume overripe roses Lisa's when she bumped against me in that tram first time geraniums in window boxes moist lumpy horseshit in the breeze a player trying to pickpocket a player how funny so I caught her hand sliding inside my coat her alarmed eyes darting up me raising her palm to my tit beneath my coat cupping it giving her a good feel only look at us that color and the world not flaring out of existence why not because you could say Excuse me Sir I'm going to nick your glasses off your nose by two o'clock this afternoon and there's nothing you can do about it because everybody's got all that information speeding in at them that's the problem which sense to pay

49

attention to because the marks have already lost their wallets watches necklaces purses before they crawled into bed last night and you ask Do you happen to have a little change you could spare Sir and most will reach into their front pockets to make you go away which is when Lisa reaches into their back ones because that's where the good stuff waits the way she feels when I roll toward her in the night her skinwarmth lips and you scan the crowd singling out the vulnerable the lost that university student over there reading while he walks that old trout nodding off on the bench the one you can tell by his walk comes from money that arrogant gait never noticed how strangers touch strangers all the time in public without realizing it arm pressed against arm thigh against thigh elbowing patting prodding a kind of unconscious communal fucking is what it is then the quick press against your pocket and your tongue between Lisa's legs giving them a brush against my teen titties while Lisa slips a purse off a mark's shoulder so casually him bumping into the cozy roundness of her heart-shaped ass me bumping into him from behind apologizing and in that sensesquall the cows never get off the thin ice and all you need is Friday Saturday Sunday everything else Lisa and the beach umbrella forest at Wannsee electric drift from club to club taking in those strippers' nakedness Café Olala Café Zeitgeist Café Elektric and beneath the table Lisa slipping her middle finger into your love is love wherever you can find it because the cross-dresser at the door answering when I asked himher saying I'm whatever sex you wish me to be sweet thing because that man in the shabby tweed is stepping right in front of you Lisa already veering in from the side you catching the scent of all those banknotes in his bloodline she dropping her steel-bead handbag oh my what a terrible bending over wallet already passed into my hand amid the Excuse-mes slipped beneath my coat and me sheering back into the crowd thinking is the new Fritz Lang movie still playing I wonder the title what was broken future zombie workers high-rise towers tasty bitch machine with that shiny—

mixed metaphor : friezes, frescoes, papa

Vladimir believes he may or may not be sitting in an elegant second-class compartment with two elegant strangers on a steam train pulling out of Alexanderplatz Station.

Perhaps he is dreaming. How, the question springs to mind, could one know? Perhaps he is really on his way to visit his mother and sister in Prague. He wants to say that is most likely the case. His mother has been doing poorly ever since his father's death. So Vladimir is leaving Véra behind in their flat on Agamemnonstraße for ten days to become his mother's son again. Walking toward her across the platform at Masaryk Station he will, as always, feel himself scrap one year's age for each step he takes. He will arrive in her austere embrace an eight-year-old boy in a sailor suit.

Still, he also has the distinct impression he hasn't yet reached his compartment, that he may be forever passing the odd chap with the ship-wrecked look braked on those stairs. Not much older than Vladimir himself, good-looking in that block-jawed, dead-eyed Germanic way, engrossed in patting himself down as if under attack by an enraged bevy of invisible bees.

There Vladimir is, contentedly automatic, locating an empty wooden-slatted seat, sliding his beat-up brown leather suitcase into the luggage rack above it, settling in for the tedious trip. There he is acknowledging with a polite smile and infinitesimal nod the couple perched across from him: the proud elderly wife with gray-bunned hair and burnished cane; the proud elderly husband with tightly trimmed gray beard and tortoiseshell glasses. They stare back at him, expressionless, making him suffer his foreignness as long as they can.

Vladimir takes out his rumpled copy of Andrei Bely's *Petersburg*, ready to revisit some of his favorite passages, closes his scratchy eyes to cleanse his mental palate, and everything liquefies into golden haze, puffy quilts, feather pillows, and perhaps the second awakening into the day (if not yet the last), into a younger, lankier version of himself sitting drowsily, not in that elegant second-class compartment anymore, but in the Berlin Philharmonic Hall, listening carelessly to his father on stage deliver some political polemics in which Vladimir is sure he should have taken more interest... and next two baritones behind him are unexpectedly joining together in the Tsarist national anthem.

He turns to see what all the vocal flag-waving is about only to find himself surveying his Berlin housing block from across Agamemnonstraße. It is a handsome corner building, courtesy of Véra's cousin Anna Feigin, whose subtenants they now are, and sticks out like a tremendous red modernist ship carrying a complex and glassy turreted structure on its bow. On each of the little balconies girdling it something green blossoms. Only the Schmetterlings' is untidily empty, with an orphaned pot on the parapet. Véra's and his two rooms (one for waking and cooking, one for sleeping and dressing) are situated on the third floor.

They have a nice view into the cobblestone courtyard with its bushy fringe punctuated by infant chestnut trees and, in the center, a faux Roman statue of Flora or Fortuna or Felicitas.

Vladimir has not been sleeping well. No doubt that is what this is all about. He is deep into the insomniac undertow of a new novel. It concerns one Franz Bubendorf, an ordinary boylike man living an ordinary boylike life who unwittingly strays into an affair with the older wife of his well-to-do uncle. Soon she (Vladimir thinks of her as a Charlotte, although he is nagged by the suspicion she may rather turn out to be more a motherly

Martha or Maria, a dishy Dorothea or Dolores) begins plotting her husband's homicide. Franz accompanies the couple on vacation to a resort on the Baltic, where Charlotte nearly goes through with her plan—having Franz row her and her husband far from shore one cold drizzly morning, helping the former boot the lout out of the boat, and letting him (who cannot, it has been foreshadowed, swim) drown in a choppy sea of revelations while Franz and Charlotte (let's call her Charlotte for now) merrily paddle toward their happily-ever-maybe.

That is as far as Vladimir has gotten.

Where things veer next is anybody's guess.

The not-knowing wakes him up every morning between two and four.

The problem with writing, Vladimir has come to understand, is the part involving writing. Ideas, characters, places, the stuff one brings into being off the page: child's play. Every sentence, however, spews a thousand contingencies ahead of it, and each of those a thousand more.

The proliferation of proliferations feels like what that odd chap in the shabby olive tweed jacket at the station must have felt like.

Vladimir has been working on the manuscript late into every night, rising each morning at four thirty to get in a few more hours' composition (shut in the bathroom—so as not to disturb Véra—cross-legged on the floor, his writing desk his valise balanced over the toilet) before setting off to earn room and board by teaching tennis to teenage numbskulls and rich philistines on the courts behind the Universum Cinema on Ku'damm. He courteously cocks his pupils' dimwitted arms for them, swings their overpriced rackets for them, scoops up their furry balls for them, talks for them, thinks for them, and encourages them to suppose they are making rip-roaring progress while he endures their assorted banalities expressed in a laundry basket of washed-out clichés.

He bolts awake, struck by the thought this awakening might simply be another false one, the next floor in some high-rise daymare, or perhaps some bottomless narcotic ocean, as if he were floating up from dark blue stratum to dark blue stratum but never reaching the undeniable surface, never emerging into the real reality.

It seems to him as if his life has suddenly grown into a mixed metaphor.

The elderly couple across from him has been replaced by twin girls in their Sunday finest, ten or twelve, smacking pink gum, fingering each other's braided bister hair, referring to each other as Miranda, and snickering over some inevitably predictable wisecrack concerning what must appear to them to be the gangly balding twenty-eight-year-old coffin-dodger sharing their compartment.

Out the train window the station's clock face (it is already ten after ten) slowly turns away from him. One by one the vault's colossal iron ribs start marching past, bearing off the depot. The platform slides past as well, carrying with it a strew of used tickets, crushed cups, cigarette butts, flecks of midmorning sunlight, gobs of spittle, and the bright aluminum flash of a single abandoned coin. A luggage cart glides by, wheels motionless, a lone red-faced passenger in an olive wool cap reading the newspaper on a crawling bench, a stall hung with seductive gray fashion magazines and piled high with pretzels and pastries, a group of puzzled people on the accelerating platform, standing still, yet striding forward, yet retreating, and all at once Vladimir is boarding a yellow open-decked bus whose first two steps are comprised of the sandy soil of Grunewald's forest—the sole spot in this umber and sooted city Véra and he wholeheartedly enjoy because of its butterflies and pine breezes and River Havel and peace and butterflies.

The forest floor dissolves under him.

He seizes the handrail to steady himself and a glottal voice—the conductor's—croups in his ear: *Up! Up!*

When the bus jerks into motion he grabs someone's shoulder but is carried along by the force of an inexorable curve, during which the whole vehicle seems to slant toward him, zooming Vladimir up another set of steps to materialize, finally, on the swaying deck.

Shakily he lowers himself onto a seat halfway back and takes in his surroundings. He is floating high above Ku'damm, the entire surface of his skin prickling. What is left of his hair dishevels in the wind.

Without warning the sun has somehow commenced setting, transforming the banal stucco ornaments along the roofs and above the entryways and balconies into translucent porticoes, friezes and frescoes, trellises covered with orange roses, winged statues that lift skyward unbearably blazing lyres.

Vladimir believes thoroughly in each floor of his dream, even though he doesn't, and when he looks again it is the middle of the night. He finds himself both lying beside Véra in their flat and strolling up a street he can't seem to recognize toward his housing block. The city is blurred by rain. His spectacles (which he didn't know he wore) are foggy. All he wants to do (and somehow with the next step he is in Prague, his mother and sister having for some reason failed to meet him) is reach his hotel to wash his face, change his shirt, and go out roaming through the old town's labyrinthine lanes that prove with every erratic turn Kafka was a realist.

Vladimir understands he is still fast asleep, has been the whole time.

Except he is awake.

He opens his eyes, which are already open, expecting Véra's soft arm lazing across his chest, but no: he is atop that open-decked bus. It is midmorning and he is in mid-Berlin on his way to Alexanderplatz Station to catch that train to visit his mother and sister in—

He rotates in his seat to seek a little solace in the substantiality of his fellow passengers' faces and is flustered to pick out, far at the back of the bus, that elderly couple from his compartment on the train.

They are squinting at him in a way only Germans can squint at others, as if Vladimir were sunlight, and the sunlight too irritatingly bright by half.

The idea skims through his befuddlement that cultivation and gentility may well end at the outskirts of this metropolis…and next two baritones behind him are unexpectedly joining together in the Tsarist national anthem.

He rotates in his seat to see what all the vocal flag-waving is about only to confront a pair of brawny thugs blundering up the aisle in the concert hall on whose stage his father is presently speaking, was speaking five years ago, will always be speaking.

As they pass, Vladimir notices the one closest to him is in the process of releasing an oily blue pistol, a boxy Korovin, from the shoulder holster inside his suit coat.

Before Vladimir can react, the Korovin begins barking in the direction of a silver-haired, silver-mustached, silver-bespectacled man sitting in the front row, the publisher and politician Pavel Milyukov.

Women cry out.

Men derange.

Chairs discompose.

In something near a single gesture, Vladimir's father steps from behind his podium, crosses the stage, leaps off, catches one of the assassins' necks in the crook of his arm, and carries him to the floor with a hollow grunt-thump.

A brief, hectic wrestling match ruptures into spacetime.

Vladimir's father is quickly on the bottom, quickly on top, straddling the assassin's chest, quickly fisting him in the temple—yet, before anyone else can react, the second assassin, the one with the boxy Korovin, aims at Vladimir's father's back and fires.

Three times.

Vladimir's father flinches and was a liberal lawyer, a statesman, a journalist.

The assassin re-aims at Milyukov. Steadies his arm. Pulls his trigger.

And nothing happens.

Stumped, he glares at Milyukov, down at his empty gun, then is beneath a heap of well-fed, well-dressed men pinning him to the floor, while Vladimir—heedless that one day, because of these sixty seconds, Véra will insist she carry her own small pistol in her purse to protect him from his reputation—watches the arched hulk of Alexanderplatz Station recede from present to preterite and thinks about how his dad died defending one of his own political rivals.

He turns back to Andrei Bely's *Petersburg* and unveils himself strolling arm in arm with his father among brightly lit stalls of the Christmas market on Gendarmenmarkt. The two are spending an uneventful evening together while Vladimir is in Berlin on winter break from Cambridge.

Their universe is tangy bratwurst, mittens, spicy glühwein, scarves, hand-carved boxes and mangers, marzipan-stuffed bread, and snow light as salt sifting down around them.

The occasion is cold, simple, superb.

Nothing occurs and that, perhaps, is best of all, for this scene merely records a son and his source wandering among droves of holiday makers who speak a language from which Vladimir can retrieve only a handful of nouns and infinitives.

The duo doesn't talk.

They merely allow the culture to lap over them until Vladimir's father halts, tugs his son's coat to get his attention, and exclaims in his ear: Why can't Russia do this?

Do what, Papa?

Invent junctures like this in places like this. Look. All these people want to be is happy. Good lord. The country's not even sixty years old. What does Germany know that we in the land of czar-fetishists don't?

Vladimir considers.

Everything, he answers.

Isn't that remarkable, his father says, genuinely remarkable, as they stray on through the laughter and chatter and cheer.

yellow : one hundred and seventy grams

Paintbrush in hand, Teresa Vogel leans back on her stool to take in her work.

And now? she asks. How does that feel to you now, Herr Köhler?

Herr Köhler sits before her in a modified dentist's chair. To be awarded the black wound-badge by the government, you have to have received one or two injuries. For the white, three or four. Herr Köhler has received the yellow.

At one point, he used to be nineteen. At one point, he used to have a family, hearing, two eyes, and a fiancée. Then he received his medal, slipped it into the underwear drawer, and became the loss of his own prospects.

Herr Köhler? Teresa repeats.

More than anything in life, Teresa wants to help people. She wants others to feel the same light from the stars streaking in at them as she does. Often, though, her mind can't seem to produce the words she needs when she needs them most. She needs some now. German becomes her second language.

Teresa began painting at the clinic in back of Charité Hospital almost a year ago, yet Herr Professor Doctor Haas still has to stop by her corner once or twice a week to remind her to make a conscious effort to look at her patients straight on.

They watch you to see how you're going to react, Fraulein Vogel. Don't let them down.

She knows that.

Of course she knows that.

Even so, she—

She was eleven when the war ended, living with her parents in the shady northern suburb of Pankow. Names of battles and numbers of dead seemed like remote disruptions, and now she is here, doing this, what she can, hating herself for her dully happy childhood, helping Herr Professor Doctor Haas and his three other assistants camouflage faces that have been partially erased by the English and French.

Christ is breathing through her underfed body as she works in The Tin Noses Shop.

Initially the team used prewar photographs to fashion the lightweight galvanized copper masks with the thinness of a visiting card.

By the time Teresa joined, the task had evolved into an ongoing struggle against chipping, bending, becoming outgrown by the patients' own shifting muscles and bones and desperation.

Much better, Herr Köhler responds at last. Smoother. Snugger.

His muffled, muddled voice makes him sound drunk.

Teresa loves him more fiercely for that, looking, explaining, looking, sensing the starlight streaking in.

I polished down the interior for a more comfortable fit, she explains, adjusting the silver wire-rimmed spectacles holding the mask in place.

Behind her a train picks up speed out of the Alexanderplatz Station.

And the hardened enamel we use now, she says. You'll find it much more durable and easy to wash. Would you like a mirror, Herr Köhler? I think you'll be—

No, Herr Köhler says. Thank you. No.

Teresa studied art in school because she wanted to learn how to become closer to herself. Her subjects were mostly generic fountains and generic busts of generic people. What she really learned in her classes was how good she was at mimicking her teachers' convictions. If that was what being a painter was about, she wanted to be anything else. And then one Sunday during his homily, her priest happened to quote a poem by the sixteenth-century mystic Saint Teresa of Ávila, Teresa Vogel's namesake, and, in the thrilling heartbeats it took him to move from the poem's first word to its fifty-sixth, Teresa's old self began to soften and evanesce. She felt a beginning followed by another beginning followed by another. Christ has no body on earth but yours, no hands but yours, no eyes with which to see but yours, no feet with which to go about doing good but yours. Saint Teresa of Ávila's language hummed inside Teresa Vogel. The more she let it populate her, the more everything else started losing mass.

That was eleven and a half months ago. The next day, one very much like this, Teresa appeared at the large clinic at the back of the hospital. She cut through a snug courtyard overgrown with ivy, took a seat on one of the green benches encircling its fountain. She listened to the water trickling and her resolve gathering.

Teresa didn't meet the doctor's eyes when he opened the French doors. She peered instead beyond the Teutonic enormity of him to take in the welcome he had prepared for his patients. The clinic was bright with flowers and flags and rows upon rows of plaster casts of masks fabricated over the last decade. On a small wooden table beside the modified dentist's chair rested a soldier's steel helmet. Its sides had been adorned with iron crosses and red biplanes, its top ingeniously converted into a clock by the insertion of two black hands.

May I help you? Herr Professor Doctor Haas asked.

I want to transform love into something radical, Teresa told the steel helmet across the room in her quiet, unfaltering voice.

Do you now? Herr Professor Doctor Haas asked, eyes blank.

And now she is here, doing this, doing what she can, having learned just how long starlight sometimes takes to reach us.

Having learned skin hues that appear just right on a drab day show pallid and gray in sunshine. Trying to imitate that bluish tinge of just-shaven cheeks turns masks into cartoons. Sometimes you need to pray very hard to sense the starlight on its way, and sometimes even then you can't quite do it, yet you must have faith the holy healing metamorphosis is racing toward you, that your visions foretell a merciful already-manifesting tomorrow.

Having learned if you don't feel you belong to the present it is because you have been put there to change it.

The only aesthetics that matter are the aesthetics of skin and bone.

Maybe later, Teresa tells Herr Köhler.

Sometimes she despises herself.

Sometimes all she wants to do is sleep.

Except then she won't be able to help people like Herr Köhler feel the inrushing rays. She won't be able, once satisfied with what she has accomplished so far this morning, to replace his mask's shed eyebrows, eyelashes, and mustache hairs, all of which she will devise out of clippings collected from the back of his neck.

She won't be able to present him with one hundred and seventy grams of kindness.

Looking at Herr Köhler straight on, Teresa feels claws dragging across her hope: no matter how diligently she paints, how diligently she shapes, glues in those fine hairs, this human stumbling through paradise will never be able to regain that slab of mouth, those teeth, that lump of tongue, right cheek, jawline, eye.

He won't be able to chew or taste or kiss.

She loathes herself for that, too, for allowing the thought to enter her head that the basis of optimism is either sheer terror or stupidity.

Sometimes all Teresa wants is to sleep until she can locate the approaching light again. That is what she will do after work today. She will bicycle back to the flat she shares with a constitutionally offended nurse and, skipping dinner, not bothering to undress or bathe or brush her sour gummy teeth, Teresa will crawl into bed and pull the sheets over her head and wait.

She would give Herr Köhler, give them all, her own muscle and tendon if it would help. She would donate her own heart if it could rid him, rid them all, of the black cysts beating inside their chests.

Now, though, looking at Herr Köhler straight on, smiling with appreciation, with admiration, Teresa Vogel hates herself and hates herself and hates herself for having learned nothing, for having learned everything, for learning that learning doesn't help, for knowing at the end of this beginning is simply another beginning and at the end of that another, and sooner or later you come to feel so used up, so empty and alone and afraid, because you finally understand beginnings are all there is.

the noise knowledge makes : a wide white splash of paint

Less than a minute and Erich Köhler has shrugged on his stone-gray military greatcoat, shaken off the delicate entanglement of bird bones in that
frightening girl's frightening hand, cut through the bright nightmare of
flowers and flags, the monstrously flourishing courtyard, and erupted onto
the street.

Hunkering down against the automobile motors and sparrow chatter and
church bells and squabble of stares, it hits him he never caught her name
and tomorrow morning he will show up for his appointment insisting he
work with somebody more qualified or with no one at all.

Erich doesn't register the bicycle rushing at him from his blind side until
its startled bell jingles and he lurches back, freezes, seething, waiting for the
angry black smudge to hurl past.

On the far side of the street he can see, if he tilts his head, a beefy bald
man in a soiled once-white button-down shirt and rolled-up sleeves urging
a group of fifteen or twenty laborers gathered around him to go on strike,
only the man's voice barely reaches him, so Erich just stands there observing
the gap of his mouth changing shape, his manic arms moving in an angry
charade.

How, he wonders, turning, trundling down the sidewalk toward the Spree, could that doctor have hired an idiot, bloated with infantile compassion, incapable of fathoming what it's like to move through the city in this smashed body?

Let *her* spend thirty seconds inside the mistake of him, hear the glass bottle shattering, the noise knowledge made as it ripped into him somewhere north of Verdun-sur-Meuse in that frosty gray dawn, damp air, back cold against the trench wall, the order to charge, the panicky scrabble from one system of belief into another.

Next nothing save his own rabbity breaths, bullets stinging past, wet slap of the round dropping the boy in front of him, beside him, and how there then visited an astonishing sense of hovering—

—clamor gone without warning—

—movement lifting away—

—the universe suddenly weightless—

—and the survivors flooding down into the enemy trench amid shouts and the gushing roars of flamethrowers.

The French soldiers were all at once on fire, their clothes, their hair, their crackling flesh, the oxygen sucked right out of their lungs, and some had already fallen backward, shrinking muscles forcing their knees to flex, fists to clench, arms to raise like a boxer's, and some still twisting in the mud, trying to scream or extinguish the greasy flames devouring what they used to be.

Those were the ones Erich went for with his bayonet, his duty to end the danger of them without wasting ammunition.

The sergeant's bellow, the scrabble, and next Erich squatted out of the March wind among a nest of smoldering corpses, opening his cigarette tin with quivery fingers to extract a Blanko, taking for granted the machine gun nest twenty meters across the demolished landscape that had been manned by Germans when his unit began its assault was manned by Germans after.

Squatting, freeing the cigarette, rising among what appeared to be a snarl of seared sculptures, smoke wisping off their limbs, stepping up onto the back of one to get out of the mud and oil reek and skin reek into that frosty gray dawn, inhaling the first hot lungful, followed by the sound of the glass bottle shattering—

—his skull coming apart—

—his field of vision bleaching into a wide white splash of paint and he awoke fleetingly, bewildered, everything canted under moonlight, lurching in the bed of an open truck piled three deep with the wounded and the dead—

—his right eardrum a high-pitched violin note, and it felt as if somebody had skinned his face while he was still alive, so he cried out in pain and awoke lying unattended in a cot in a long dark corridor, other soldiers mewling around him, and maybe it had already been a month, or only an hour, it didn't matter, because Erich was struggling to breathe through layers of bandages, and someone nearby was begging for help, and a surgeon was standing there, asking: *Can you understand me, Private Köhler? Nod if you can understand me—*

Erich cried out in pain and *You're home and in good hands*, the surgeon was saying. *Your fiancée knows. Your parents. There will be a number of operations. All of them will hurt like hell. I wish I could tell you otherwise. We will give you painkillers. They won't work.*

Over the following weeks Erich tried to will himself to die, but his heart was too emphatic, his lungs too committed to swelling and sinking, and he awoke in the middle of the night, small yellow bulb throwing the room lined with beds into a swirl of gigantic shadows, listening to a conversation between maybe two orderlies, two cleaning girls:

Ghastly. Look. They don't got no profiles. It's like apes—all bumpy foreheads and slits for noses. Why keep them miserable things alive?

At the clinic a poker-faced technician took the impression for his mask while explaining some of the benches in the nearby park were painted light blue, code to mothers for which to avoid with their children, and that's where he could sit, anytime, for a think, but not on any of the others, that was against the law, and afterward the poker-faced technician shook his hand, wished him luck, and sent him on his way.

Nothing could prepare Erich for what squinted back in the first hand mirror he held up, how people went out of their way not to touch him, how once a week he was forced to join a group of the blasted for Hamster Trips—forays into the countryside to scavenge for food, dig up roots, pick berries, do whatever it took to avoid the white-hot shame of those lines sponsored by the local churches, those patronizing smirks from women spooning out watery potato soup into tin bowls.

I'm more whole than you, those self-satisfied Christian smirks said—*more giving, more devout, and I love you with all my heart because I know what happened to you happened for a reason because God knows everything and can do everything and that's why there are influenza epidemics and children with bone cancer and babies born without brains because He is our sun, our refuge, our rock.*

Fuck you, Erich saying under his breath, seething, trundling along the fecal Spree, *fuck you and fuck you and fuck you and fuck you too you little self-serving shits.*

reds

newsreel : two

Emelka Corporation

presents

—TODAY'S MOST THRILLING NEWS—

~ AVIATION'S FIRST TRANSATLANTIC PASSENGER ~

The future arrives in Germany !

American millionaire Charles A. Levine

HIS PLANE PILOTED BY DAPPER

—CLARENCE CHAMBERLIN—

lands in *EISLEBEN*

surrounded by 50,000 cheering souls !

Adventures abound on the way from

AMERICA !

COLUMBIA'S *nonstop flight*
—6,285 kilometers—
—44 hours, 35 minutes—
A COMPLETE SUCCESS !

~ GERMAN CRUISERS TO THE RESCUE ~

Warships battle ice to aid imprisoned vessels !

Thick floes prove no match
for our BRAVE FORCES
IN THE BALTIC !

You can be sure they'll get through
with FOOD & FUEL for the starving crews
of the merchant craft
held fast by the FROZEN SEA !

~ OUR NATION'S FIRST WHOPPER DIPLOMATIC BALL ~

Berlin hosts CRÉME DE LA CRÉME !

Look at these distinguished
Ladies & Gentlemen !

Smile for the CAMERAS !

GOVERNMENT OFFICIALS

lance olsen

DIPLOMATS
LEADERS IN THE ARTS & SCIENCES
attend a SPECTACULAR ball
IN OUR ELEGANT CAPITAL !

~ JAPS "FEED GODS" IN WEIRD FESTIVAL ~

WHAT A CURIOUS SIGHT !

OVERJOYED by bumper crops
our friends in the EAST
place gifts at the feet
OF THEIR BIZARRE DEITIES !

Have you ever seen
—*such strange rites ?*—
—*such mysterious dances ?*—

73

blue : a chair is a very difficult object

Walking, Mies concludes as he watches the fecal Spree slide by his cab, is—

I never—

That is a building.

I never walk.

Look at the building.

(The efforts of the mystics remain episodes.)

We must have—

There is a man.

There is a building.

Look at the man.

That building is—

Order.

One could say Berlin is a captive of
the nineteenth century.

The broad boulevards.

Massive stone façades.

That poor man.

The neo-Grecian pillars.

Neo-Roman arches.

Look at his face.

Look at—

One could say I always take—

(Every How is carried by a What.)

We must have order.

It can be no other—

What was wrong with his face?

Because the word *rectilinearity* exists.

I always take taxis back and—

There is a building.

Perpendicular.

(Every force evolves a form.)

Because a taxi is—

And so I rarely see a city.

What is there to see in a city?

Is that a—

Berlin: the imperial hallucination.

(One should never forget a square is also a rectangle.)

In the end the war being a failure of German architecture.

A taxi is a moving room.

Because red is—

There is a building.

Because red is money.

Because we can.

Have order.

Because a civilization must.

Have it.

(The guilty accuse themselves.)

Who said—

A motorcycle bombinating past.

The clean line feels like time travel.

I miss my wife.

Bombinating.

All this moving.

Otherwise we would be something else.

I love her but I cannot live with her.

Because less is—

Blue.

I can live with Lilly but I cannot live with Ada.

my red heaven

We must know that life—

Silver.

We must know that life—

I can live with Lilly now but I could
not live with Ada then.

Her chairs.

This sky: that blue.

But later it will rain.

They say.

Because red is money and yellow is
also money.

Because what would it feel like to
know your son's name?

His uncluttered substantive.

What would it feel like to—

All this moving.

Lilly's chairs untaught me so—

There is a building.

If God exists, he is—

I changed my own.

Name.

The sound of *Mies* stretching into the
sound of—

There is a—

Thank you, Lilly.

There is another.

The sound of *Mies van der Rohe*.

Will they ever stop?

When in doubt, deploy the Dutch.

Whisper of the aristocratic.

If not, perhaps, the substance.

Because my father carved stone.

Because when in doubt check on the
streetcars in Berlin.

Because one must do what one must
do in order to enter certain circles

(Every human being has the right to pure color.)

Because the important thing in any crisis is whether the streetcars are running.

Kingdom of Prussia.

Because if the streetcars are running, life is bearable.

Lilly's furniture hurts, the lines are so impeccable.

Because the phrase *industrial steel* exists.

Plate glass.

(Because every architect has been or will be a refugee.)

(This is a self-evident truth.)

(We become exiles in our own countries.)

Because my father carved stone and I carve space.

(We become exiles in our own—)

The efficiency of skin.

My son carves—

(That man's face.)

Specialists are people who repeat the same errors.

Martin used to say.

I hear you, my father's last words, deathbedding, *but I haven't crossed over yet.*

Just a moment.

Just a—

Then the elated smile spreading across his was-ness.

New York: a beautiful catastrophe.

Berlin: a doomed Pompeii.

The will of an epoch translated into three dimensions.

We must understand life cannot be changed by us.

(A chair is a very difficult object.)

Light and—

There is a—

A house is a machine for living in.

Said Le Corbusier.

His name eleven letters and one lack.

Mine fourteen and three.

And they came to me and said: *Design a memorial for those two.*

Gimpy Rosa Luxemburg.

Scrawny Karl Liebknecht.

And so life will be changed, but not by us.

To Rosa: *Kindly stand still while we beat you with our rifle butts and shoot you in the head.*

Lilly.

Her chairs designed in wind tunnels.

Because less is—

To Karl: *Kindly step out of this moving*

vehicle while we shoot you in the back.

Ada.

Because the space between buildings is—

They execute people in front of brick walls.

Because the space between build-ings is as important as the buildings themselves.

So I built a brick wall monument.

Cantilevered slabs.

Steel-and-concrete frame.

Jagged bricks.

Grout unsanded.

Because one could say—

All this moving.

Because one could say the clean line represents a choreography for living.

A way of maneuvering through presentness.

If God exists, he is—

Architecture starts when—

Architecture will always be the real battleground of the spirit.

—God is in the details.

Speechlessness sans silence.

Because architecture starts when you carefully put together two bricks.

And so they ask me: *What do you talk about when you're with a client?*

And I tell them: *Never talk to him about architecture.*

That's the crucial point.

Talk to him about his children.

About his rust red and dark chocolate Italian loafers.

Talk to him about—

About—

water lily : flames inside a telephone

Nearly seven hundred kilometers southeast of the taxi in which Mies van der Rohe rides, in a warm pasture overlooking the Austrian village of Stockerau, six-year-old Ernst Herbeck nibbles a long blade of grass, back against an oak, inhaling the loamy moistness of cow patties, daydreaming of Berlin.

He has never been there.

He will never go.

He has seen photographs.

He was too young to remember them.

Behind Ernst's gingerbread eyes Berlin exists as a baroque palace spreading out from the city center in concentric wrinkles like a pebble dropped into his imagination. Every corridor branches into ten. Every week it is larger than the week before. There are more statues than bubbles in a bottle of seltzer. In one room everything—chairs, sofa, desk, bed, lamps, walls, floors—is fashioned from amber, in another gray-scaled snakeskin, in a third South American butterfly wings. One tilts at a forty-five-degree angle so that whoever enters becomes woozy and one has been fabricated into a giant snow globe where shreds of newspaper fall ceaselessly from a specially engineered ceiling.

Nibbling a long blade of grass on a low hill overlooking Stockerau, Ernst doesn't see the eggnog church tower hatted with an asparagus-hued onion-bulb belfry. Doesn't feel the acorns knobby under his rump. He isn't listening to the herd of cows crunching hay methodically at the far end of the pasture or the minor turbulence of older boys playing somewhere in his vicinity.

Ernst is swaddled in himself, aware he has located a window and climbed through it into this summery Fridayness.

Monday and school and the bigger boys who because of his cleft lip shove him when they pass by on the streets and who because of his lisp call him Lizard Mouth are solar systems away.

All Ernst perceives are the pretty words fluttering in his head like colorful clothes on his mother's laundry line:

Rhinoceros.

Water lily.

Lemon are many blue leaves and—

—and how are we today? scrunch-shouldered Horst asks, welling up like a comic-strip genie. Enjoying our afternoon?

Horst is one of the schoolboys who pick on Ernst. Horst reminds him of a cross between a pig reared on its hind legs and a pit bull. More than twice Ernst's age, Horst's face is a mayhem of pink cream-tipped pustules, his hair cropped lice-short, his eyes two black pencil erasers.

Hi, Hortht, Ernst says.

His attention slides to the side, beyond Horst's quantity, realizing the bigger boys he half-heard playing somewhere nearby are no longer playing somewhere nearby.

They are playing with Ernst.

That's when Dieter, long-limbed and buck-toothed, steps out from behind the left side of the oak and Joachim, stumpy and blank-faced, steps out from behind the right.

Ernst feels himself hoisted off the ground.

The long grass blade falls out of his mouth.

Well, this is fun, says Dieter.

Joachim's laugh sounds like a fish bone just caught in his throat.

In school Ernst has come to understand very little about reading, writing, or arithmetic. He has come to understand very much about how when older boys commotion into your life there is nothing you can say that won't make matters worse. When older boys commotion into your life, it isn't time to struggle. It is time to relax. Soften your muscles. Let your arms drop and close your eyes and let the next thing take place.

This afternoon Horst, Dieter, and Joachim have decided to employ a good length of braided rope to hang Ernst upside down from a tree to see what happens.

Once Ernst is dangling between Dieter, who has hold of his right ankle, and Joachim, who has hold of his left, Horst ties a hangman's knot and slips it over Ernst's feet. He tosses the other end of the rope over a thick branch three meters up.

Ernst feels himself rising higher.

An orange, yellow, and green sentence drifts through his mind:

Mothers see inside time.

Look how red he's getting, says Dieter.

That's purple, Joachim corrects.

The blood vessel in the middle of his forehead, says Dieter. Can blood vessels explode?

Everything can explode.

Let us pray, says Horst. He lowers his head: To every thing there is a season. A time to choke and a time to struggle helplessly. A time to lisp and a time to be punched in the chest.

Ernst's curiosity gets the better of him and he squints open one eye to see Horst's black pencil erasers examining him with scientific curiosity.

Ernst shuts his eye again.

A time to be tripped and a time to fall. A time to be tied up and a time to be lifted unto heaven.

(*The wind of fairies.*)

A time to be force-fed cow shit and a time to puke out your guts.

(*The cry of violets.*)

A time to be slapped and a time to be wedgied.

(*The cry of violets in language rain.*)

A time to—says Joachim, trying to join in. A time to—
Jesus Christ, says Horst.
Give me a second, Joachim says. You always—
Just make something up, for fucksake.
A time to be chased (*Bells, the world looking different.*), Dieter goes on, and a time to be wet-willyed. A time to be kicked in the nuts and a time to be—Look. His nose is running.
These are truly gifts from God, says Horst.
Do you think he's crying? asks Joachim. I think he's crying.
You idiot, Dieter says. Your nose always runs like that when you're hanging upside down.
Call me an idiot again, Joachim says.
A time to—

(*These flames inside a telephone.*)

Go ahead. See what happens.
A time to—
Do it, Dieter. Call me an idiot. Go ahead. Do it.
You fucking, fucking idiot, Dieter says.

Joachim and Dieter roll in shade among the splash of acorns, Joachim's arms clamped around the top of Dieter's head, legs around Dieter's middle. Dieter has reached up to yank a fistful of Joachim's hair. Joachim has become a clown with a squeezed-up face and a wide-open mouth. Horst has meanwhile stepped to the side, inspecting the scuffle before him with the same look fathers adopt when informed by their sons' teachers their offspring will grow up to become sponges.

When Ernst opens his eyes again the pasture is empty except for that herd of cows crunching upside down at the far end of a flat green cloud.

The sensation in his fingertips is gone.

His vision pulses white and black.

Ernst isn't sure if the something whirling across the pasture toward him is inside his head or outside.

The something appears to be a miniature tornado, a dark havoc of shingles, planks, rake, wheelbarrow, shoal of leaves, broken windowpanes, cuckoo clocks. He shuts his eyes and the something boils over him and there emerges amid the flying debris that mustard-breathed doctor from Graz who will try to fix Ernst's cleft palate and fail and Ernst working in a munitions factory the moment he realizes he can no longer hear his own ideas so a polite young attendant in a white lab coat attaches cool electrodes to his temples and into his brain rages a surge of deafening red followed by that nice man Leo Navratil welcoming him to the Maria Gugging Psychiatric Clinic near Vienna where Ernst will live contentedly for the next thirty years because Leo one morning will hand him a blank postcard-sized piece of Bristol board and ballpoint pen and ask him to write down what he sees behind his eyes and Ernst will accommodate Leo because writing is the most wonderful feeling in the world and he wants to share it with everybody he has ever met and everybody he has not even though twelve hundred stylized eagles are dripping fire from their talons onto a burning city below and Ernst can make out women with their babies clutched to their chests and men with their arms over their heads and children not yet teenagers collapsing in the immolation ocean and—

—and, just like that, Ernst's future has roared passed him.

Dangling, he blinks into the warm summer stillness.

Reaches up to rub his runny nose.

A plan evolves inside him.

He tightens his tummy and performs a capsized touch-your-toes. When he flops back down again, muscles unqualified for the job, he depends there, catching his breath, marking time, until he starts hand-over-handing up his own prickling legs, flops back down, starts hand-over-handing, flops, starts once more, watching the splendid words in his head holiday and depart:

Panther.

Sour cream.

Please hurry now, Lord.

Please hurry and get out of my mouth.

mother, child : art doesn't help

Nearly seven hundred kilometers northwest of the tree from which Ernst Herbeck lolls, you raise your head from your tidy work desk in your nearly empty studio and spot a taxi two floors below rumpling over the cobblestones on Weißenburger Straße.

The profile of the passenger balloons up succinctly—jowly, fleshy nosed, protruding lower lip—perhaps smoking a cigar stub, perhaps picking at his thumbnail—and the taxi enters a flickering perplexity of sun and shaggy branches and the passenger elapses and then the cinnabar-and-black car itself. There is the sharp amazement of it, the sense you might have passed that man on the street yesterday, pass him on the street tomorrow, yet would never know it, never have an inkling about what he does or why, and, that notion dissolving into the sun-and-shade dazzle quickly as the taxi itself, you lower your head and return to the limestone slab before you.

This afternoon you are making a lithograph of a mother and child.

In the far corner one of Beethoven's piano sonatas plays on your gramophone, birthday present from Karl.

Your subject—late twenties, hair pulled back into an already-graying bun, purple veins cobwebbing her cheeks and forehead—stepped out of the main gates of the Schultheiss-Patzenhofer Brewery two blocks over. It was the end of the day shift. You often stroll by about that time searching for all the ways grace can reveal itself. Most of the men and many of the women in your tenement, in many of the tenements that make up Prenzlauer Berg, work in that brick building the color of stoneground mustard. Midsummer, when the breezes stop, the factory's hot yeasty fumes accumulate in the streets, cling to everything—bedding, towels, clothes, furniture, hair.

You often recognize your neighbors among those coming through the gates, people you nod to every day in the stairwell that smells like the inside of a cardboard box, queue with for the toilet on the dark half-landing, the locals with whom you chat in the waiting room of Karl's medical practice around the corner.

This woman's face caught you because of the stubbornness and tenderness and fatigue in it. You approached her, asked if she might be interested in posing. Just fifteen or twenty minutes, you promised. Just a few drawings.

Rather than slowing down, over her shoulder she asked how much.

Last Sunday afternoon you met her in the small park across the street. You didn't expect her to turn up with her three-year-old son, chubby cheeked, mussed hair, wearing miniature overalls. You told her your name was Käthe. She told you hers was Helga.

Helga took a seat, her boy leaning into her. You carried most of the conversation, squatting before her, trying to get her to relax. Her boy loosened into sleep while Helga replied in monosyllables. She seemed both defiant and suspicious of you and your peculiar undertaking. Why would someone fritter away her time like this when there was so much honest work to be done?

You made several hasty sketches in your pad and thanked her.

The second your money touched her palm, you could make out some part of her click off and begin gaining distance from you even before her body moved.

Draping her groggy son over her shoulder like a lazy cat, she turned and left without saying goodbye.

Somehow you always find yourself making lithographs of mothers and children. You keep circling around the theme, returning to it as though someday you could get it right if you just kept at it long enough.

Over the years you have learned to work the way a cow grazes.

Rush, and all you do is make mistakes faster.

The stickiness of your grease crayon, tang of your black ink, smooth movements of your hand: that's it; that's all; that has to be enough.

Once you had the audacity to believe you were some kind of revolutionary. In your childhood dreams, you died a hero on barricades. Perhaps you believed too long that humans were heading somewhere. But when your son. When Peter. When only three months after the war had. That's when old age commenced flourishing inside you. The news from Flanders crashing in. You were forty-six. No. Forty-seven. You finally recognized all armies were simply postponing the end of the world from one day to the next. Every war carried within itself the war that would answer it.

Karl Kollwitz was a teenage medical student when you met him. He wore his dark Van Dyke and silver pince-nez with elegance, was a committed socialist, a member in good standing with the S.P.D. You were Käthe Schmidt, a person you have come to consider a sister from whom you have slowly drifted apart over the decades. It proved easy to admire Karl, and next adore him. He proposed and you said yes and he asked what he could give you, how he could help your art. You started to love him when you moved to Prenzlauer Berg and he decided to dedicate his practice to the needy. You did, too, in a way, documenting those who lived around you. Karl built a studio for you, the one you are sitting in. He hired Sonya, your live-in housekeeper. You loved him even more when you found yourself pregnant with Hans, and four years later Peter, and instead of your production slowing down as you eased out of your twenties with two boys and a husband in tow, it sped up. But when something. When Peter. When it storms back at you, you feel all your strength scraped out. It was the news from Flanders. It was the hours. It was—

You can make another lithograph of a mother and child, a thousand of them, yet you will never get any closer to your dead son, your progressively distant husband, your youth. Art doesn't help. That's the hardest lesson you've had to learn. People insist art makes things better. You prove them wrong every day. Art doesn't make life more bearable or longer or impervious to anguish. Its real goal is the opposite: to teach you nobody can be saved in the end.

You watch the muscles fidgeting beneath your hand's skin, can't believe that thing belongs to you: crinkled, blue-veined, brown-spotted. You don't know how you can bear it that your Peter's death will persist for the rest of your days.

You were twenty-two. You were forty-seven.

You were sixty.

Your fingers have fattened. Your knuckles have swollen. And still: you're somehow also enchanted by it all. You loved your husband and then the hours came and now it may be called something else, yet it is also somehow deeper than anyone could have told you. You are thankful for that, for how sometimes Karl's large pudgy hand searches out yours and squeezes in the middle of the night and in your half-sleep you are staggered by the exquisiteness of his touch.

The sonata, it comes to you little by little, is done, has been done for—

How long has it been done?

The needle scratches and ticks at the end of the record.

Another sound prompts you to raise your head and look out your window. Below, a trio of musicians has set up on the sidewalk at the park's entrance. A thickset middle-aged woman in a flowery dress hugs a banged-up raspberry accordion. A young thin black man in a bright lemon shirt, noisy red scarf, baggy black pants, and noisy red suspenders accompanies her on banjo. A slightly shorter young man with long greasy ash-colored hair plays horn. They are in the midst of an out-of-sync rendition of some Dixieland jazz number, at their feet an open suitcase stuffed with—what are those? Clothes to sell? Tablecloths? Towels?

Two little boys, eight or nine, trot down the middle of Weißenburger, scouting odd chunks of coal that have fallen off delivery trucks, dropping them into a burlap bag sagging between them.

You listen, trying to recall the name of the piece. You heard it for the first time with Karl at the club a few months ago. It was your birthday, that evening you caught a glimpse of Bertolt Brecht, short and gangling, slouching in the back with his too-thick eyebrows and truck driver's cap and black leather jacket, sucking at his Havana cigar.

And then you have it: *Basin Street Blues*—and Sonya is tapping on the door, asking if you would like your afternoon coffee.

It's two already? you ask, turning to find yourself looking, not at Sonya, but at a human collage—a nose, a bit of cheek, a rectangle of shoulder, a triangle of gray-blue dress, a ruddy hand.

(All these years, and you still feel awkward around her, unsure how to carry yourself, make small talk.)

Five after, Frau Kollwitz, she says. Perhaps something sweet to go along with it?

Sonya won't enter your studio unless you invite her. You won't invite her because you want to finish your lithograph before Karl returns from the clinic.

What do we have?

Shortbread. Coconut macaroons. Perhaps a—

Apfelkuchen?

I haven't been to the bakery yet. I'm just going soon as I—

Don't trouble yourself. Coffee.

The door clacks shut discreetly.

Sonya—

The door cracks open discreetly.

Do you hear that music? you ask.

The jazz. Yes. Would you like me to go down and tell them to—

You wouldn't happen to know if it comes with lyrics, would you?

Lyrics?

Sonya stalling a second, a second more, and—

swimming : look at the—

—and Frau Kollwitz doesn't even know, does she, how could she, not my place,
believing I'd swim through those piano notes forever, studying in Salzburg, Vi-
enna, forming the quartet, drizzle in cream, back again, knowing more about
music than she ever, Salzburg, Vienna, Berlin, and then the convulsion, good
word, who could have, quartet survived, me too, if you can call this, on with
your coat, check for keys, down the stairs, into the jazz, *can't keep tempo, can*
they, playing twice a week, me, small halls, *good life, can't deny it, restaurants,*
weddings, but this negro music, and look at that woman, *glamorous white*
parasol, even in Weimar, yes, Liszt himself, Schiller, Goethe, breathing them
in, live by your lessons, look at her with the what do they, pixie cut, *takes*
some getting used to, new breed, secretaries, *that's what they're, good money if*
you can, nylon stockings, *honorable life,* hand cream, *knows where she's going,*
Nivea, *once to an audience of two hundred fifty, opened the paper one morning*
and everything, toast, jam, my cash useless, value gone, hunger upon us, what
did Liszt, life one long and bitter suicide, *what words,* one long and, *think*
of it, father's telegram: Lost fortune last night= =Vati=, *one world x-ed out,*
another scribbled in, you can smell the brewery, can't you, wet bread, negro
music, load of chaos, but those flower stalls, how they, you play notes and then
they're gone, can't get them back, not the same, not ever, but that orange tabby,
cat queen of the shop stairs, classifying me with its Egyptian wisdom, yellow and
pink flowers, roses, don't embrace how long something lasts, who said, embrace

its intensity, yet carnations, orchids, because sometimes all that's left is to enjoy them, the stalls, everything in its place again, even that white Pomeranian, don't see many of them anymore, old woman with rhinestone leash, too late for her, lucky to have had them, the years, my piano, those notes, all these lives taking place around me, frantic score, Apfelkuchen and marzipan, and one day nothing but turnip coffee, muscle pudding, fake honey, call it a, one long, *and there, what is it, conch ashtray in the, what does it say,* Our future lies in the air, *Zeppelin quote, Count Ferdinand, white broomy mustache, and those two coming toward me, older gent in an oversized worn black, short brown fringe of hair, look at his shiny head, long ears, hands behind back, banker, philosopher, sneezing, doesn't cover up, good God, think of it, sneezing, dirty Jew, younger gent on his left in a less oversized black, full head of dark, what kind of animal does he, listening, head lowered, look at these hands, mine, good God, those darling plastic butterfly napkin holders in the shop window, scrubbing floors, rinsing dishes, paying the baker with* her *money, proper sweet to go with the, like nothing ever happened, just two men passing, never glancing in my, nothing to see here,* phrase the art of not drowning *passing between them,* a-chew, *already behind me, tin of hand cream, saved for it, my own cash, Nivea blue and white, yet her,* a-chew, *her son, wears his not-ness in her eyes, what was his, Hans, no, that was the other one, no matter, gray eyes, gray hair, gray skin, gray face round as one of those she's always, only she doesn't,* a-chew, *farther down the street, that's the secret, every drawing a drawing of her drawing herself, how could I ever be interested in a man who could be interested in me, nice view of the needy out Frau Kollwitz's window, and me knowing more about music than she ever, yellow and pink and purple and scarlet, that's the important, I knew things once, eighth note, cloud shreds, rain later, knew things, get on with it, only this spring afternoon, this stroll, straightening your back, raising your chin, opening the door to the shop, stepping through its tinkling bell, warm gust enveloping, cinnamon, chocolate, raisins, rye—*

soundtrack : none

FADE IN:

CLOSE—ABSTRACT RUSTLING MOTION RESOLVES INTO LEAVES SHIMMERING IN BREEZE THROUGH TREES ON STREET IN PRENZLAUER BERG. BELOW OCCASSIONAL CAR OR BICYCLE PASSING. PEDESTRIANS.

SOUNDTRACK: NONE.

WITH TITLES.

DISSOLVE TO:

1. EXT. SHADY SIDEWALK—DAY

PAN DOWN SLOWLY—

SECRETARY with pixie cut walking rapidly by flower stalls.

DISTINGUISHED OLD WOMAN waiting for her white POMERANIAN to finish peeing against black park gate.

Three LABORERS in wool caps, wrinkled shirts worn outside pants, open jackets, heading to work.

                                                        DISSOLVE TO:

2. EXT. OUTSIDE PARK ENTRANCE—DAY

STREET MUSCIANS playing. Thickset MIDDLE-AGED WOMAN in flowery dress on accordion, thin YOUNG NEGRO on banjo, slightly shorter YOUNG MAN with long greasy hair on horn.

CLOSER – Musicians' faces feigning good cheer for tips.

                                                        DISSOLVE TO:

3. EXT. INSIDE PARK—DAY

CHILDREN playing tag around benches and through bushes, laughing.

                                                        CUT TO:

4. EXT. RACING TRAIN—DAY

TRACKS blurring beneath TRAIN on outskirts as it rushes toward thriving capital to deliver goods.

CLOSER—COAL SMOKE shooting back over stunning complexity of gears and wheels.

DISSOLVE TO:

5. EXT. TIDY APARTMENT BLOCK FAÇADES ALONG WEIßEN-
BURGER STRAßE—DAY

ROUND-FACED OLD WOMAN with gray hair pulled back in bun
opens window wide from inside second floor.

CLOSER—She leans out, stares down at jazz musicians.

DISSOLVE TO:

6. EXT. BAKERY—DAY

BAKER throws bucket of water on shop's steps, brushes them down
with broom.

DISSOLVE TO:

7. EXT. AERIAL SHOTS—DAY

From low-flying ZEPPELIN sliding over city. Emphasis on bustle.
TRAIN YARDS, BOATS PLYING CANALS, BRIDGES SPANNING
MEANDERING SPREE, POTSDAMER PLATZ, CATHEDRAL, BRAN-
DENBURG GATE, and, finally, REICHSTAG emerging through TIER-
GARTEN woods.

DISSOLVE TO:

8. EXT. WEIßENBURGER STRAßE SIDEWALK—DAY

CAMERA TRACKS frumpy MAID in light-colored open coat revealing her dress and white apron. She passes TWO MEN.

Deep in conversation, the men don't notice her.

CAMERA REVERSES COURSE to TRACK the TWO MEN. ARNOLD
SCHOENBERG and ALBAN BERG, both in dark suits. ARNOLD still
the brilliant teacher, bald and in his fifties, gesticulating. ALBAN
still the faithful student, ten years younger, wavy dark hair.

CLOSER—

>ARNOLD
>[TITLE:]—Calling what I do "atonal music" is
>like calling swimming "the art of not drowning."
>I just want a little—

ARNOLD flinches into a SNEEZE without covering up.

>[TITLE:]—sorry—pollen—clarity in sound. Like
>your wonderful Wozzeck.

>ALBAN
>[TITLE:] Nothing outdoes the joy of adding
>another unplayable work to the repertoire.

ALBAN and ARNOLD laugh.

>[TITLE:] Six years visiting your flat
>taught me every—

ARNOLD

[TITLE:] I taught you how to remain poor
a little longer and how to play Ping-Pong
tolerably well.

ALBAN

[TITLE:] How to continue our war on the
French kitschmongers.

ARNOLD

[TITLE:] Ravel. Bizet. Did you read the
Deutsche Zeitung review of my violin
concerto? "Schoenberg's piece combines
the best sound effects of a—"

ARNOLD flinches into a SNEEZE without covering up.

[TITLE:] "—of a hen yard at feeding time
and practice hour at a busy music conservatory.
The effect is that of a lecture on the fourth
dimension delivered in Chinese."

CUT TO:

9. INT. FACTORIES—DAY

Interiors as artworks (sans people) around Berlin. Emphasis on
SPEED, MOTION, GLEAMING MACHINERY, SYMMETRY, DESIGN.

CLOSER—whirring pinions, sprocket wheels, etc.

CUT TO:

10. INT. BANK OFFICE—DAY

Large room packed with SECRETARIES typing at rows upon rows of uniformly arranged desks. Visual symphony of matching clothes, hairstyles, gestures.

CLOSER—Their HANDS like pianists' traveling deftly over keyboards.

CUT TO:

11. EXT. STREET SHOTS—DAY

BUILDING FAÇADES and CONSTRUCTION SKELETONS (sans people), not as edifices to live and work in, but rather as amalgam of Neoplasticist horizontal and vertical lines (Piet Mondrian's paintings, only in steel and concrete).

DISSOLVE TO:

12. EXT. WEIßENBURGER STRAßE SIDEWALK—DAY

ARNOLD and ALBAN's walk, continued.

> ALBAN
> [TITLE:] After Wozzeck's premiere they wrote:
> "I regard Herr Berg as a musical swindler
> and artist dangerous to the community."

ARNOLD

[TITLE:] Let them eat Einstein.

Laughing, ARNOLD and ALBAN pass a few SWASTIKA-CARRYING YOUTHS with heavy cudgels loitering on the street corner. The youths are too involved in their own conversation to register the composers.

ARNOLD

[TITLE:] Stupid bulls. Trust me. Their
slapstick won't last.

ALBAN

[TITLE:] If it's art, it's not for them.

ARNOLD

[TITLE:] If it's for them, it's never going to be art.

ARNOLD flinches into a SNEEZE without covering up.

CUT TO:

13. EXT. U-BAHN/TRAIN STATIONS—DAY

CROWDS from every walk of life spilling out/in, many catching sight of camera and staring into lens, self-conscious, wary, as they hurry along.

CUT TO:

14. EXT. FACTORY SMOKESTACKS—DAY

SMOKESTACKS belching raw energy into cloudless sky.

CUT TO:

15. INT. PUBLIC BATHHOUSE—DAY

CAMERA PANNING through ROMAN-RUSSIAN BATHHOUSE festooned with geometric mosaics under skylight ceilings. MEN lounging in white towels and robes around swimming pool. WOMEN in dark one-piece bathing suits in and around large sunken tub.

DISSOLVE TO:

16. EXT. PARK—DAY

ARNOLD and ALBAN enter PARK, choose vacant bench, sit, enjoy the children playing tag. ARNOLD leans back to take in the sun.

CLOSER—

ALBAN
[TITLE:] We've got life. Those bulls
don't. Our profession. Wives. Children.

CLOSEUP—

ARNOLD
[TITLE:] Last night I told Gertrud not to
trust me. We were having dinner.

ALBAN
[TITLE:] But you're utterly faithful to her.

ARNOLD
[TITLE:] I was trying to be as honest as my
music.

CUT TO:

17. EXT. TEMPELHOF AIRPORT—DAY

CAMERA locked above right wheel and struts of silver plane building speed on runway.

Take off.

Ground falling away.

CUT TO:

18. EXT. TEMPELHOF AIRPORT—DAY

Lifting, PLANE soars over camera at end of runway.

CUT TO:

19. EXT. TEMPELHOF AIRPORT—DAY

CAMERA locked above right wheel and struts of plane turns capital
below into Cubist patchwork.

CUT TO:

20. EXT. POTSDAMER PLATZ—DAY

TRAMS, CARS, HORSE-DRAWN CARTS, BICYCLES, PEDESTRI-
ANS—all synchronized by TRAFFIC POLICEMAN (seen from behind) with angular, automaton arms motioning.

DISSOLVE TO:

21. EXT. PARK—DAY

ARNOLD and ALBAN on bench, continued.

CLOSEUP—

> ARNOLD
> [TITLE:] Gertrud told me she loved me.
> I don't know why. I told her how glad I was
> we were—

ARNOLD flinches into a SNEEZE without covering up.

> [TITLE:]—were together and not to
> trust me.

> ALBAN
> [TITLE:] I don't understand.

> ARNOLD
> [TITLE:] I love you at this precise second,
> I said. If you died tonight it would feel like

someone had torn out my organs.

PAN BACK to take in TWO SERIOUS YOUNG BOYS striding in front of ARNOLD and ALBAN. The boys are carrying neatly packed bundles of LAUNDRY to deliver.

ARNOLD and ALBAN pause to watch them go by.

ARNOLD proceeds.

> [TITLE:] Ten years ago we were other
> people. Ten years from now, ten weeks,
> ten minutes—who knows?

> ALBAN
> [TITLE:] Music and love play the
> body like instruments.

> ARNOLD
> [TITLE:] I don't want to be an emotional
> plagiarist. I don't want to steal other
> people's tenderness or hurt and absorb it
> into my own until I can't remember
> whether it's mine or not.

CUT TO:

22. EXT. TIERGARTEN—DAY

WELL-TO-DO WOMEN AND MEN riding HORSES on paths through trees, two by two.

CUT TO:

23. EXT. TELEPHONE SWITCHBOARD—DAY

CLOSEUP—MYRIAD OPERATORS' HANDS, one set after another in quick DISSOLVES, racing back and forth to connect megalopolis to world.

CUT TO:

24. EXT. POTSDAMER PLATZ CLOCKFACE—DAY

CLOSEUP—CLOCK HANDS on grassy island in middle of Potsdamer Platz, whirling FAST-FORWARD deliriously.

CUT TO:

25. EXT. CITY PALACE—DAY

MILITARY MARCHING BAND, PARADE, FULL POMP as HEADS OF STATE exit through palace's main arch to line of WAITING CARS on boulevard.

CUT TO:

26. EXT. PARK—DAY

DOGS ON LEASHES tearing at each other as their OWNERS hold on, watching neutrally, BYSTANDERS taking bets on winner.

CUT TO:

27. EXT. WEIßENBURGER STRAßE SIDEWALK—DAY

MAN IN STRAW HAT lighting cigarette while examining three identical MANNEQUINS in pixie cuts and flapper dresses posed in shop window.

DISSOLVE TO:

28. EXT. PARK—DAY

ARNOLD and ALBAN on bench, continued.

CLOSE—

> ARNOLD
> [TITLE:] Now, I said. This second.
> That's all I can truthfully promise.

ALBAN lowers his head, pondering, then raises it again, says—

> ALBAN
> [TITLE:] The twelve pitches of the
> octave will always be equal. Never an
> absolute up or down.

> ARNOLD
> [TITLE:] People who laugh haven't yet
> received the terrible news.

Camera PANS BACK SLOWLY as ARNOLD and ALBAN sit side by side, laughing in hazy sunshine.

DISSOLVE TO:

29. EXT. PARK—DAY

REVERSE OF FIRST SHOT: LEAVES shimmering in breeze through trees obscures into ABSTRACT RUSTLING MOTION.

DISSOLVE TO:

30. EXT. AERIAL SHOT—DAY

ABSTRACT RUSTLING MOTION resolves into shot from LOW-FLY-ING ZEPPELIN sliding over PRENZLAUER BERG.

DISSOLVE TO:

31. INT. ZEPPELIN—DAY

CLOSE—

20-YEAR-OLD MAN in light wool jacket, black scarf wrapped loose-ly around neck, black hair combed straight back, sits alone at table draped with white tablecloth by window in airship's stately dining room, cradling coffee cup in palms, attending city below.

if god : a hundred different movies

How the silvery afternoon light makes the tiny people in the park below sparkle.

Those children-glitters convoluting through hedges.

Those—what are they?—men? women? lovers? pals?—scintillating on that bitsy bench.

Sprites, he thinks to himself, taking another sip.

Sprites, Billie Wilder thinks to himself, taking another sip of cappuccino one hundred and fifty meters above the capital.

The flight from Hamburg will have lasted just over ninety minutes—the length, it strikes him, of a perfectly structured movie.

Billie didn't sense the launch. He doesn't sense the gradual descent. He won't sense the landing. The yellow pencil next to the black leather notebook before him on the table is one hundred percent immobile.

This is what travel on an airship feels like.

It feels like a decade from now.

Like all you have to do, if you don't want one second of your life to be that second, is pay enough.

His notebook carries a calculus of scribbles for an article he's writing, a piece for a local tabloid about the more than twenty-five women who have gone missing on and around Kurfürstenstraße over the last three years.

All of them destitute.

Most of them hookers.

Some of the women men.

Billie sees the work he is doing as part of a larger unfolding.

That's why he didn't attend the University of Vienna, despite his parents' urging. His studies would have taught him nothing about how to become Billie Wilder. He moved to Berlin instead and found a job as a stringer for several papers and as a taxi dancer, the guy hired to Foxtrot and Lindy Hop with customers at ballrooms around town.

Billie's decisions have never been shortsighted.

Billie has always taken the long view.

The tiny park among the tenements beneath him has given way to the brewery has given way to the bridge, which bridge, he doesn't know, and up here the silvery afternoon light is different. You can already smell a green dampness in it, the approaching rain. It crosses Billie's mind that he will turn twenty-one in twelve days.

He takes another sip of cappuccino, luxuriating in the swallow, and deliberates on whether he should have ordered a slice of Sachertorte with whipped cream to accompany it.

This stage of his life is all about keeping pace with his plans. People who don't care about the later stages of their lives will at some point in their twenties begin to sense themselves losing velocity, settling for less, landing in a field of comfortable mammalian dormancy.

Billie sees it taking place all around him.

He can't evoke a more terrifying sensation than augmenting inertia disguised as maturity and contentment.

Next thing your children are scrabbling all over you as you try to read the newspaper, from time to time in their narcissistic restlessness indifferently snotting on the back of your hand and trampling your balls.

Max and Eugenia, bighearted people, his father, his mother: Billie tries to forget them a little more every day.

They own the cake shop in Sucha's train station surrounded by the rolling hills of northern Austria. They wanted Billie to work with them, take over the family business with his brother, forge a sense of familial continuity, financial security.

You'll be happy, they said.

They said: The shop will always take care of you.

Billie canceled his train ticket and treated himself to this voyage—his first on an airship—to remind himself where he is going and what getting there will feel like. For his twenty-first birthday, he will treat himself to Emilie, his favorite transvestite. He reserves Emilie for special occasions: the day he could stop work as a stringer and begin work as a regular for the tabloid, the small but significant raise a few weeks later, each step he has taken away from that cake shop in that ho-hum station.

Inspecting the two men at the table across from his—the aging panda with flabby hands and goldfish eyes unblinking behind gold wire spectacles (he's the one doing most of the talking); the overly attentive young lemur with women's hands and nervous eyes rapidly blinking behind heavy tortoiseshell spectacles (he's the one doing most of the listening)—tuning in and out of their conversation, Billie decides it was a good idea not to order the Sachertorte.

He needs to watch his cash with the little things so someday he can afford the big things.

He needs to follow the blueprint.

The five-year program.

The ten.

If you don't want to inherit the shop, his parents argued, at least get an education. Learn an honorable profession. Become a businessman. A lawyer. You'll never want. Everybody will respect you.

Billie chose Berlin because he heard you can become anything you want there.

If Berlin were a part of speech, he heard, it would be a transitive verb.

He chose taxi dancer and stringer, confident in five years he will have become something else.

In five years he will have become a screenwriter and director.

Because, as his father always said, if the rich could hire the poor to die for them, the poor would make a very nice living.

Awash in clinking silverware, chinkling stemware, animated prattle, shifting chairs, random coughs, and, all at once, a butterfly (Billie catches sight of its iridescent blue wings flattened against the drapes above panda and lemur), his thoughts bend toward how there is something unimaginable about them, the transvestites, about their glamorous bothness and neitherness, their soft faces always just shaved for you, powdered with soap-scented makeup, how their long-fake-nailed fingers around you are at the same time muscular and delicate, one thing and perpetually something else.

Without blueprints it is like trying to run on the floor of a lake in lead boots. Nothing happens as you and everything else use you up.

Without blueprints you wake up one day dating a nice Jewish girl. Next thing you know you've married her. And then you're rocking someone's baby in your lap. It turns out to be yours. You're rocking two of them. You blink and it's three, and your forward momentum is spent.

You feel yourself falling asleep and you know you will remain that way for the next twenty-five years.

A quarter century.

Half your life.

When you wake up again, you'll be dead.

When you wake up again, you'll think: If I were twice as smart I'd be an idiot. Your children are grown, gone, don't particularly like you, never have. That's the great lesson. It's what children do until they themselves have children and fall asleep for twenty-five years and wake up dead, regretting their disinterest even as they come to understand their own children are already grown, gone, don't—

But Emilie's hair is long and ash blond and she smells like cigarette smoke and alcohol and extravagant violet perfume.

Billie can't get enough of the thrilling confusion every time he raises her dark green mesh flapper dress with the black beaded deco design and jagged hem and lampshade fringe and asks her to keep on her stockings and dark green high heels.

That dissonant shock is like watching the first few seconds of a hundred different movies back to back to back.

He was born Samuel but his mother nicknamed him Billie. He doesn't know why. Billie is convinced one day he will travel to the United States. He will drop the *ie* at the end of his name and add an American *y* and compose a screenplay about the magnificent confusion he revels in with Emilie.

It will be a romantic comedy called *Some Like It Hot*.

Perhaps it will be set in Chicago. Perhaps it will be peopled with gangsters.

(Everybody likes Americans.)

(Everybody likes gangsters.)

Billie has promised himself he won't start until he has learned his craft. Right now he is trying to figure out how people really talk—no, not how they *really* talk, but how they really *should* talk when they begin talking in feature-length movies, which will be any day now, everyone knows it.

More than anything Billie wants to engineer impeccably clipped lines like: *I don't go to church. Kneeling bags my nylons.*

Nobody sounds like that in real life—but they would, if real life were as interesting as a film.

If God lived on Earth, Billie's father used to say at dinner after balancing his books at the end of the month, people would break His windows.

The morning Billie left home, his mother hugged him so hard something in his lower back made a cracking sound. His father slipped him some cash in a sealed envelope, shook his hand, and whispered: Don't forget, son—no matter what, you have to believe in yourself, despite the evidence.

A week later Billie was trolling Kurfürstenstraße for a hooker. Everyone said the ones there were cheap, friendly, clean, and ingenious. Billie had been walking half an hour in dim light across the street from a Neo-Renaissance villa that people in the neighborhood pretended was the private home of a banker but knew was in fact used as a secret gambling club frequented by aristocrats, intellectuals, and rich lawyers.

His plan was to sweep together enough courage to approach one of the teens that were actually teens rather than one of the thirty-year-olds pretending to be teens.

Then Emilie's ash blond hair reaching all the way to her collarbone and her long black fake fingernails and her black lipstick and black eyeliner and white makeup and dark green flapper dress and matching high heels.

Emilie met Billie's eyes as he passed.

Next thing it was an hour later.

In reality it will take Billie another twenty years and more than fifty screenplays before he is ready to begin *Some Like It Hot*.

He will be fifty-three when the film premiers.

Right now, though, is for figuring out what he believes about moviemaking.

For starters, he believes if after one of his pictures people sit down and talk about it for five minutes before they reenter their lives, he will have succeeded.

He believes Fritz Lang and Robert Wiene are jerks for overdoing it with the fancy shots that distract the audience from the plot and characters.

Shoot a couple scenes out of focus and win a foreign film award.

Big fucking deal, believes Billie Wilder.

Standing in dim light across the street from the villa, Billie explained to Emilie he had no idea what he was doing.

Don't worry, honey, Emilie said. Just leave everything to me.

They agreed on a price and Emilie took Billie's hand and led him back to her room in a tenement two blocks away: a fifth-story jail cell, unpainted, saturated with the odor of chlorine and clammy mushrooms. On the floor in one corner lay a thin narrow mattress, next to it a tin washbowl, water pitcher, and blotchy washcloth the color of a smoker's teeth.

There was no electricity, only an oil lamp on the floor that made the room shiver.

Two of the windows were nailed up with boards.

For a while they sat on the bed and kissed.

Emilie reached down and started massaging Billie through his trousers. She unbuttoned him, eased him out, and took him into her warm moist mouth.

Billie remained convinced she was the most desirable woman he had ever met until he whispered for her to keep on her stockings and high heels and raised her green mesh flapper to her waist.

That's when he began watching the first few seconds of a hundred different movies back to back to back. He saw an older version of himself boarding a train for Paris, a ship for New York, a plane for Hollywood. He saw his first wife and their little daughter accompanying him. He saw his second wife before she was his second wife stepping onto the film set and the set reshaping itself around her. He saw the same hands that helped his mother knead dough in Sucha, touched his daughter's soft cheek with amazement every morning, and brought his last trembling glass of water to his own ninety-five-year-old lips, reach out one evening in April, 1961, to accept a gold-plated statuette for best picture on a brilliant stage teeming with applause, listening to the disorders wonder makes inside your head, thinking: It's true—the more flesh you have, the more the worms will have to eat.

sixty four : americans dressing poorly

Your system, as I understand it, categorizes sixty possible types of sexuality. Is that correct, Herr Professor Doctor Hirschfeld?

Sixty-four.

And it is your belief in this profusion that led you to establish the First Congress for Sexual Reform in—the young lemur checking his notes, blinking rapidly—1921?

It is this demonstrable phenomenon that has guided me through my entire career.

What would you say to those—

The inverse is also the case, naturally: the woman who needs to be liberated most is the woman inside every man. Let me—the panda with walrus mustache stopping when he notices the waiter hovering beside him, saying—nothing, no—presenting him with a soft open palm.

Just the bill, please. Together.

Let me mention in this context our country's recent penchant for Naturism. There is no greater pleasure than lying on a beach, naked, surrounded by others lying naked, absorbing the sun's primal force. This serves as an important reminder to us all that we are made of blood, bones, and flesh, and not some bourgeois finger-wagging.

Scribbling shorthand in a brown leather notebook.

The panda patiently waiting, then waiting less patiently.

I believe you were about to ask what I might say to those who disagree.

I was going to ask what you would say to those who believe such sexual profligacy adds up to a rather extensive list of human perversions.

My categories celebrate Western culture's concept of human potential. They offer a paradigmatic corrective to a rather pervasive if inaccurate impulse toward sexual dichotomization. More simply put: imagine how monotonous life would be if we all possessed the same beige urges.

Nature's reason for such variation would be—

The categories' reason for existing is that they exist. I am merely pointing out what others have either failed to notice or repressed.

Does it therefore follow that one should extend what you term "civilized compassion"—the waiter returning, bill sleeping on a small silver tray in his hand; the formal presentation; the lemur rooting for his wallet—that one should extend such "civilized compassion" to, say, rapists and pedophiles?

My goal is to nuance the world, not dictate its laws. Nor is detecting antisocial, violent, predatory instincts in some categories reason enough to extrapolate those impulses to all.

From your perspective, then—

From my perspective it is easy to love from a safe distance. Our clergy and moral philosophers show us how to do so daily. The more difficult formation of the emotion—the one simultaneously involving loathing, approval, excitement, encouragement, commitment, revulsion, faith, longing, fear, lust, empathy, ecstasy, pity, hate, unbounded generosity, and so on—exists as a spiky complication. Unfortunately, that complication can't be summarized by means of Biblical banalities.

You would offer, therefore, that sexuality is—

Sexuality is a chance. This is why it was important for me to situate my Institute at the edge of the Tiergarten—within sight of the Reichstag. There it performs the work of symbol. It houses a full library and the Museum of Sex, a clinic affording medical consultations for adults, and *The Journal for Sexual Knowledge*, to which Herr Professor Doctor Freud himself has been gracious enough to contribute.

This sounds very much like social progress.

My Institute even provides rooms in its villa to remarkable visitors who would like to stay with us a little while in order to delve into our ideas more deeply. You may be familiar with one of your colleagues at the *Frankfurter Zeitung*—Walter Benjamin?

I'm afraid not.

We have received the utopian thinker Ernst Bloch and the French novelist André Gide, the esteemed Russian film director Sergei Eisenstein and Berlin's very own cabaret singer Anita Berber. In fact—was that *a butterfly*?

A butterfly?

Yes. I'm sure a blue butterfly just flew over your head.

I don't—scanning.

It must sense the world the way many of us do, conceiving the airship in its entirety, whereas there stretches out a vast planet beyond.

Americans have begun to refer to you as The Einstein of Sex.

Americans dress poorly. I visited once, delivering a few lectures, and confess I found the lot of them far too happy. Aggressively so. They say thank you too often. They smile without cause. I believe it was their own Mark Twain who once suggested God created war so Americans would learn geography.

I wonder if—a startle of silver sunlight sheening the restaurant's interior, the slight down-tilting of the airship's nose—the lemur squinting out the window—Ah, we're landing. I very much appreciate you taking time out of your busy schedule to answer a few questions. If I'm not overstaying my welcome, perhaps one final one?

Naturally.

How would you describe our current zeitgeist? That is, what makes our age, which you are documenting with such thoughtful precision, different from those that have gone before?

The panda dipping his head, straightening his spectacles—his head raised by an idea—Have you heard of Wang Lun?

I haven't.

Executioner in the Ming Dynasty. He was famous for the alacrity with which he sliced off his victims' heads. The convicted party would climb the steps to the scaffold, kneel, and, before he had wholly located himself, the sword whooshed and the deed was done. Everyone admired Wang Lun's skill. And to be sure he was proud of his own work. Nonetheless, he possessed a further ambition. He wanted to decapitate a man so skillfully, so gracefully and swiftly, that the severed head would actually remain on the victim's neck. Well, it came to pass Wang Lun was required to carry out twelve executions in a row—a particularly laborious undertaking, as you can imagine. He used the ordeal to hone his skills, improving his craft just a jot more with each coup de grâce. When the last of the dozen prisoners started to climb the steps—a gentle bump, barely noticeable, and out the window the ground crew tugging at the thick ropes, far along into the mooring process, the airship slowly finding gravity—Wang Lun fell in behind him, raised his sword, and sliced through the prisoner's neck so delicately, with such artistry, that the man didn't notice. Rather, he continued climbing the steps to the scaffold as if nothing had transpired and, at the top, turned to complain to his executioner. "Why do you prolong my agony?" he asked. "You were merciful with the others. What have I done to offend you?" Wang Lun smiled at him and replied in a humble voice: "You have done nothing to offend me, sir. Please: kindly just nod in approval of my art, and we can begin."

grays : greens : whites : blues

newsreel : three

~ ANOTHER COLUMBUS TO SAIL WEST ~

But this time
THROUGH THE SKIES!

World's *LARGEST AIRSHIP* under construction
in *Friedrichshafen am Bodensee*
LAUNCH SET FOR NEXT SEPTEMBER!

Tickets go on sale soon:
UNITED STATES!
SOUTH AMERICA!

lance olsen

NORTH POLE !

A true *MAMMOTH* of the heavens:
—236.6 meters long—
—top airspeed: 70 knots—
—2,650 horsepower—

YET ANOTHER *SUCCESS* FOR OUR
GREAT NATION !

~ GERMANY'S EINSTEIN OF SEX ~

Or so our AMERICAN friends call Berlin's
Herr Professor Doctor Magnus Hirschfeld !

WELCOMING SCHOOL CHILDREN
to his WORLD-FAMOUS
Institute for Sexual Research
in OUR NATION'S CAPITAL !

Look at these curious
Boys & Girls
filing in for their first lesson about
the Birds & the Bees !

Smile for the CAMERAS
Herr Professor Doctor !

~ HUMAN ZOO IN HAMBURG ~

WHAT AN EXOTIC SIGHT TO BEHOLD !

ELECTRIFIED by what awaits them—
crowds STREAM into the EXHIBITION HALL

A UNIFORMED BRASS QUARTET PLAYS

Mighty **TARZAN** *bends metal rods*
with his **BARE HANDS** !

– FAT LADY RIDES HORSE LED BY MIDGET –
—*PINHEAD CLOWN can't stop laughing*—
—*ADORABLE INDIAN CHIEF* twirls his lasso—

HUNCHBACKS, ALBINOS, AFRICANS !

Have you ever SEEN
—*such BIZARRE spectacles* ?—
—such *FANTASTIC* FREAKS OF NATURE ?—

~ **WHO'S THE MOST BEAUTIFUL OF THEM ALL ?** ~

LOOK AT THESE DARLINGS !

Munich judges have a hard time choosing winners
in *Germany's*
PERFECT BABY CONTEST !

Wouldn't YOU, too ?

EVERY ONE

AN **ARYAN**

KING OR QUEEN !

when it happens to you : little white commas

The iridescent blue butterfly flits free of the airship and is catapulted high into the silver light by a rogue gust of wind.

The gust stirs up time around her. In the boil she sees the middle-aged woman with a limp she used to be. Her name was Rosa Luxemburg. Rosa had come to conclude over the course of nearly five decades that the most revolutionary thing you can do is simply say aloud what is taking place in the vicinity of your life. The first president of Germany disagreed and ordered the Freikorps to help her become inconspicuous.

They showed up in the night, goons in paramilitary uniforms, brought her to a small windowless cell in the basement of a building, and began asking her questions to which she couldn't know the answers. When she told them the truth they slapped her. So she began to lie. They yanked her hair and punched her in the breasts.

After a while they jerked her out of her chair and shoved her into the hallway, where a rifle butt flew from the darkness and slammed into the side of her face.

She sprawled on the concrete floor, dazed.

The tip of the rifle barrel pressed into her left temple.

An instant before Rosa Luxemburg turned into a butterfly, she thought: *When it happens to you, it's not a story anymore.*

After, she watched from above as two goons grabbed what she had once been by its feet.

The thing's faded grayblue dress hiked up under its armpits, bra and soiled panties bared. The goons dragged it through the corridors and up a staircase to the backseat of a waiting Opel.

The Opel drove south through the city. One goon sang a song under his breath. Rosa couldn't make out the tune. They passed along dark streets, over a bridge, by buildings containing newspapers, publishing houses, warehouses.

Half an hour later, the car drew to a stop beside the Landwehr Canal down the block from the Gleisdreieck U-Bahn Station.

It was cold and hard to make out what was going on.

They hoisted Rosa's history from the backseat, roped a heavy chunk of cement around its neck, and rolled it down the canal's sloped walls into water the shade of outer space.

A splash came.

A splash went.

Forty-seven years slipped beneath the surface and maybe this took place eight years ago, maybe eight-tenths of a second.

The problem for the blue butterfly was that time had stopped feeling like time.

It felt more like whitewater looks.

Like everything and nothing is occurring at once and it's all rushing furiously but not getting anywhere and everybody is an outcast from themselves.

Who knows? the rabbi once told Rosa when, as a little girl, she had approached him one Saturday after services. Maybe souls of righteous Israelites go to a place not unlike goyim heaven when they die. Maybe they are reincarnated through many lifetimes. Maybe they just wait until the coming of the messiah. And maybe the souls of the wicked are tormented by demons of their own creation or cease to exist altogether. How should I know? You think I took a vacation to Death and sent back a postcard explaining everything? You're ten, Rosa. Live now. Worry later.

It is a bright morning and she is five, the doctor announcing to her parents (as if Rosa Luxemburg were deaf) that the child's hip is tubercular and she must be confined to bed in a cast for one year.

It is also a gray evening and rain puddles along a dingy street. The air is heavy and wet. A licked-iron tang from the factories burns the back of Rosa's throat.

She is nine, a block away from her tenement in Warsaw, late for supper. She knows she will get in big trouble if she isn't home soon, yet she can't seem to locate the alley through which she usually cuts. She is close. She can sense it. But it's never the next turn, never the one after that.

Church bells gong six o'clock. Her father will yell at her. She can see him. She can see her mother sitting at the kitchen table, watching his tirade as if there were nothing she could do about it.

He will call Rosa stupid.

He will call Rosa lazy.

Done, he will send her to bed without any food.

So she hurries along, limp-running, doing the best she can, everything around her ordinary and terrifying.

It is also night and Rosa is standing in a deserted potato field. She is twenty-six. The field sheens with pearly frost. A man appears in front of her near a derelict shed. Although Rosa has never met him before, she knows his name is Ulrich.

Ulrich is a comrade, someone she's supposed to meet here to plan the next step in the revolution. Singing that folksong, "Abandoned, Abandoned, Abandoned Am I," Ulrich steps into the shed, shuts the door behind him, and the shed explodes in a silent inflation of white light.

The blast expands until it loads the sky with a diaphanous silver—the same sky into which she has just been catapulted by that rogue gust of wind.

Below slides a jumble of redbrick church spires, elevated railroad tracks, neighborhood parks, waterways, tarred rooftops.

Rosa can't identify any of them.

She can't fathom where she is or where she's going.

On several of those rooftops she spots the dead starting to gather even though it won't be their time for hours. Some have known for a year and a half what comes after, some five seconds: just more dyings, one after another, like Russian nesting dolls, until death gets tired of you and finally walks away for good.

They are standing with their arms by their sides, faces tilted up, waiting for not-time to pass.

And then, fast as it welled up, the gust carrying Rosa is gone.

A large green island shaped like a snail crawling down the middle of the River Havel slingshots toward her.

Little white commas fleck the water—*boat wakes*, that's what they are, Rosa sees—and a small white castle with an iron widow's walk spanning two turrets on the shore, and Rosa is among a flurry of tree branches, coming to rest on the tip of a tall blade of grass in a wide meadow.

She takes a moment to compose herself. Breathing heavily through the series of tiny openings that run along the sides of her body, she resolves she will rest here. It has been nothing if not an arduous journey.

As she tucks back her wings, a black shadow scrambles across the grass around her and flickers out.

Rosa thinks *cloud*.

She reflexively raises her head to see the sole of a heavy brown boot rushing down toward her. She scarcely has an instant to recognize this second death as a friend before the dreams start over again.

algebraic sentences : among them, dandelions

Elderly Anton and Julius decide on a whim to veer from the gravel path
the color of shortbread winding through Pfaueninsel and cut across the
meadow behind the imitation castle ruins.

They have made it into their eighties, wear loose-belted, box-pleated,
wool Norfolk jackets (Anton's chestnut, Julius's olive), matching wool trousers, heavy brown boots. For them almost every day has become a cold day.
Inside their boots their toenails are yellow and flaky. Inside their trousers
their legs mottled and purple-veined. Anton and Julius have watched themselves with curiosity and dismay impair into themselves.

A retired sommelier at a posh hotel just off Ku'damm, Anton sports
abridged gray hair, round spectacles with blackened lenses, a briar pipe. A
retired concierge at the same, Julius sports no hair, no spectacles, no pipe.

They walk arm in arm as they have walked arm in arm every pleasant
day for more than half a century. The gesture became reflexive long ago,
a means of closing the distance between their hearts. Over the last fifteen
years—ever since Julius's tremors slowly began taking hold and Anton's
vision slowly began emigrating—it has developed into a necessary act of
shoring up against what the years have taken from them.

Julius is doing no more than rejoicing quietly in the sun's heat upon his face,
absent-mindedly recalling a song popular when he first met Anton on a

break in the alley behind their job: Crimson roses gem the heather, blushing in the clasp of May—or was it June?—May or June—woods and vales and something something echo back the something else. Julius hums the melody under his breath. It strikes him the German Empire wasn't even three years old when someone made up those lyrics. Wagner was busy building his opera house in Bayreuth, Schliemann poking through the clutter of Troy, Thomas Mann's algebraic sentences only an indistinct discomfort in Júlia da Silva Bruhns' belly.

Anton is doing no more than drawing pipe smoke into his mouth, letting it suffuse across his tongue, up into his sinuses, releasing it into the abundance of the audible world.

Years ago he forgot how to remember the colors blanching out by degrees around him, the lights everywhere growing auras, the nights getting darker, the days twilighting away.

Anton could see.

He could see he saw less.

He could differentiate nothing besides pastel blobs and blurs.

He took continual solace that it could always be worse.

Unfailingly, it will be.

But for the present it is these sharp peacock cries reaching him from the far side of the island, and, closer, small-bird cheeps and trills and a little boy's practiced whine for ice cream and his father's fierce comeback and footfalls crackling across gravel.

For the present these short blusters of Nordic breeze among swishing branches and a squirrel's rustle and the sandpapery sounds of a gardener's tools working loam.

Across the meadow a group of young women and men are laughing, single words rising up from their exchange into the afternoon—*clover*—*goose shit*—*licorice*—and, closer still, the inexpressibly crucial noise of Julius's voice humming out of tune something Anton can't place.

Anton raises his right boot to take another step through the puffs of scruffy meadow grass only to encounter himself on break in the alley behind the hotel at which he used to work. It is 1872, and he is striking up a conversation with Julius, who has just asked if he could bum a cigarette off him, yet the conversation has already ended and Anton barely remembers anything about it except its exhilaration, because he was hired last week and—and it is a month later—how did that—Anton's job neutralizes his days, contracting each into a succession of fussy demands, sullen looks, finicky complaints, and pasty faces, exactly like the day before, only lost a little faster—it is a month later and Julius and he are stepping off the boat onto Pfaueninsel on their first date, tentative, unsure where this thing might lead, their surroundings prickling with prospects, and—wait—they are on their fourth outing, not their first; their sixteenth, not their tenth—except they haven't met yet, and Anton is still a little boy, his mother holding him by the wrist on a street corner outside a candy shop, bending over and wiping smeared chocolate from his lips with her own spittle wetting a handkerchief—the soothing smell of it mingles with her lavender perfume, her pushy fingertips—wondering why he is passing the same candy shop as a different person, the one who just spent his first night with Julius, the city bleared by rain, his spectacles foggy, him wanting nothing save to reach his own flat to wash his face, change his shirt, give himself over fully to the experience of jumbling into romance, believing it will be gone within a week, a weekend, even as he suggests a de- licious light-bodied Pinot Noir from Italy to a swollen pig-eyed businessman and his ringlet-haired daughter—or is she his mistress?—and—no—that was later, he is sure of it—now he is strolling through the stalls of a flea market along the Spree with another man, younger, svelter, beautiful, blond—his name is Siegfried—no—Joseph—no—Walter—it's not a man at all, but a girl named Lucie or Gretchen or Sonja, and Lucie or Gretchen or Sonja is carrying two long-stemmed roses with which Anton souvenired her as they met outside the Savignyplatz Station, Julius startled by how serious things have already gotten, and—how did that—time is hurling past—their stroll is already over, has been for more than half a decade, Anton's shoulder leaning into Julius's as they sit side by side in a pew in the cavernous Berlin Cathedral, attending with closed eyes a brilliance by Bach, the what is it called, the one everyone knows, toccata and something, that one, toccata and something in something, realizing at any juncture—the very next one—the very next out-of-control thought—his lifelong companion could be buried, realizing if he, Anton Schaeffer, born and raised among Spandau's cannon foundries and gunpowder factories, had never been on this planet nothing very much would have changed, not about that, not about anything, Julius would simply have found somebody else to love, the hotel somebody else to serve its patrons, and even his mother would have wiped chocolate off somebody else's filthy toy mouth—and sight comes—and sight goes—and nobody really cares except you—for others it's just an anecdote, something to tell their friends about before taking the next sip of Chardonnay—one day Anton Schaeffer could see, they say, and on another he couldn't, how sad and do you think it will rain again tomorrow—no—wait—it is two years from now and Anton is wandering into their cramped kitchen in search of an apple, will wander into their cramped kitchen in search of an apple, only to hear Julius leaning over the sink, swallowing what Anton at first presumes to be pills for his tremors, and he stepped up beside Julius, will step up beside him, to give him an impulsive hug, only to discover they aren't pills at all, no, but rather copper-coated pfennigs, Julius's hand shaking so awfully the water in his glass is sloshing over onto the linoleum floor, was swallowing, is swallowing, will always be swallowing coins, one after the other, and Anton instantly felt, will instantly feel, exhausted, emptied, overwhelmed, and, looking up at the ceiling to collect himself, consider how best to respond without upsetting his lover, his boyfriend, his hope, he saw, will see, has always seen death as a towering wave of black fire crashing down on them in very slow motion.

Off the grass, please! the gardener shouts at their backs.

Anton brings down his right boot on a butterfly (although he doesn't register the dainty crunch one hundred and seventy-two centimeters below his current thoughts) and without turning raises his hand in acknowledgement of the gardener's command as Julius begins steering them back toward the shortbread path.

The couple steps through a swarm of gnats busying their faces.

Anton declares: A telling.

What?

Give me a telling.

Now?

Yes.

Right. We—yes—we just walked through the most heavenly patch of tiny white flowers.

Describe.

A light snow spread out across the grass. Among them, dandelions.

Describe.

The meadow?

No.

The dandelions?

No.

The color yellow?

Yes.

…

…

I can't. I'm sorry.

What else do you have?

Do you remember the lilacs we used to buy at the shop down the street?

I wonder why we stopped.

You said the smell didn't count without the rest of it.

I said that?

Yes.

I was wrong.

And a single giant gnarled oak.

Just passed?

Profuse vines covering the trunk.

Profuse. What a word. Next to the folly?

Of Roman ruins.

And?

The Havel, blue under sun, gray under cortical clouds. Plush villas on the far shore set into the tree line.

Swans?

Five or six. In the water. Seven. A white wedge gliding.

And *that*.

Animal in the undergrowth.

No. Another.

Wheels?

Yes. Gardener's wheelbarrow?

Pram. Girl. Early twenties. Alone before a hedge. She's stationary, staring ahead, mouth open slightly like a turtle, as if stumped, rolling the pram forward an arm's length and back with all the anger and disappointment of a short lifetime built into the action.

The elation of bringing another indulgence into the—

Anton bark-laughs.

Julius joins him.

They give each other's arm a squeeze and advance toward the dock where a boat, then bus, then train will carry them back to 52°30'04.6" North and 13°18'12.4" East and an orange tabby named Oscar Wilde.

walking damage calendars : a radiant system

And what can I get you two gentlemen? asks the man in the bratwurst hut on the far shore.

Unshaven. Sinewy root network neck.

Ordering, Julius's heart extends to include him.

Carl Fischer thinks *blind*, listening to worldwhir. *Fairies.* Then about this evening. Finishing up here in an hour, dropping by the local Lutheran church on his way home to help out with chores—mopping, hauling a few boxes up from the cellar—and next off to the public bathhouse, nice shave, Kurfürstenstraße. He likes approaching the young ones most, the girls who look least like they have it all figured out. They can't quite sense how different he is from the rest. Whores in their forties, fifties—you can hear the desperate thrum in their voices wrecked by cigarette smoke as they tick through their prices. They would go just about anywhere and do just about anything for just about nothing. Their missing teeth. Thickening waists. How they have become walking damage calendars.

Coming right up, sir, the man says, adds: Gonna love 'em—plucking two from the grill—Extra juicy. Made fresh this morning.

Amateurs believe the young ones taste best. Certainly funnest to truss on the kitchen floor. All that terror in those wide eyes. Older types—they get it right away, give up on the spot, like belief was a beautiful way to live until the facts bolt in.

Specimen of the true German spirit, Julius thinking with a gust of pride.

Conscientious.

[In their surrender, you can smell how death lives in clocks.]

Methodical.

Movements grounded on firm, reliable philosophical principles.

Because hunger spilled out into the streets after the war. Nobody knew what to do once most of the horses were gone, the dogs, cats, rats. Nobody except Carl Fischer. That guy had a plan. Got a head on his shoulders, thinks Carl Fischer, applying the mustard.

[The neural rush.]

[The radiant system.]

The funnest being The Hogtie. The always-welcome surprise of the unexpected transvestite. The static on the mattress, sock-stuffed mouth, clumsy drag toward the tub. Smoked pork for the butcher shop. Fat into soap. Bones into buttons. Spare bits into the Spree. The concept being economy. Being you pay your rent on time and the landlord couldn't give a shit when the neighbors complain about the banging. Carl Fischer has a business to run. He has things to do. The point of him giving a shit is what. Weight of number so-and-so in your journal. Description of. Funnesses had. Date. Yield. Accounts receivable. Never easy, but continually rewarding. Scholar of meat. Equipment. The slender names. Stainless steel knife. Gambrel and winch. Hacksaw, bucket, grinder. Simplicity of the hammer.

Julius begins counting out his pfennigs at once to give himself a few extra seconds to do the math and outwit his unsteady fingers.

[The stun strike. The flinch.]

Lovely day for a stroll, isn't it, piling plates with potato salad. Moving to the tap with two mugs. Rain tonight, though, they say.

[That shuddering release.]

The funnest being The Hoist. The Scramble. That's when everyone becomes special. The search for the breastbone, insertion of the knife just above it, the twist, the tug, the slice from sternum to groin. Every slice

Julius looking skyward.

141

Anything else for you gentlemen?

Saying no. Saying thank you.

Brief bow of head, friendly grin, before turning his attention to the next customers: chubby mummy, bull-chested daddy, and that boy who was whining for ice cream back there, yes, that's the one.

And what can I do for you today, sir? the man asks the boy brightly, bringing his parents appreciative smiles.

gives rise to new faith. The dying are always dangerous, their quick thrashing, and next it is the stench, the mass of bloody brownish entrails tumbling out over your feet, across the floor of the tub. You kneel, dig through them on your hands and knees for a trace of thereness, an inkling of apocalypse. Split the breastbone, extract the remains, take your time disconnecting the head, removing brain chowder, eyes, tongue. Take your time cutting the ham, the shoulder, the chops, the tenderloin. Yet in the end all you ever uncover is another example of averageness—this heart, these lungs, these kidneys, this slippery liver in your cupped palms. Your people could be anybody. They are anybody. Their skin sacks carry no important news. Everything stays itself. A body disappears piece by piece and what is left is this—this heap, this sludge of bits and liquids. And that's what you have to settle for, over and over, because the only thing you've ever learned is the ecstasy of patience.

Carl Fischer thinks *breeders*, thinks *litter*. Then thinks about something else. Finishing up here in an hour, dropping by the local Lutheran church on the way home to help out with chores—mopping, hauling a few boxes up from the cellar—and next off to the—

red hair, redshift : the space between notes

—concert. When was—With Schnabel. Artur. Sonata in—Mozart's music the color of good hefeweizen. Artur struggling to be patient with me before that face-ocean. Yet no one can deny socks are cotton jails for the feet. Furrows gathering across his brow. Beneath this tree. Beer and B-flat in hand. Two sweet old men over there taking their seats. Teeteringly. Look at—One on the right—You can never play Wolfgang Amadeus cynically. Artur's forehead becoming a rumpled sheet before he—Because time exists so everything doesn't happen at once but everything happens at once anyway. Look at their—Trouble with socks is they get holes in them. Artur stopped mid-phrase, hands lifting from the keyboard, glaring: Can't you *count,* Einstein? *The face-ocean hushing to see what would misoccur next. A beat, a beat, and me replying:* Whatever is worth doing is worth doing badly, wouldn't you agree? *The laughter heaving. This table. This afternoon. Sometimes all you can do is be grateful. Otherwise life with socks is a scandal. Because combing your hair takes time. Living like yourself takes sixty or seventy years. Sunlight prickling with electromagnetic radiation and the uncomplicated contentment of joining Christmas carolers with your violin outside your apartment door. That warmth among others. After-dinner snow. Lone flakes hanging in the—Neighborhood a different—Sounds softened. Silver light emanating not from sky but street. Memory a form of falling. You share your whole life with a corpse that shares your name. Because the point is I feel lonely only with other people. Because the photon starting at the center of the sun*

and changing direction whenever it encounters a charged particle takes between ten thousand and one-hundred-seventy-thousand years to reach my eyebrows. And when I sit all I want to do is walk. When I walk all I want to do is be back ho—Can't you *count,* Einstein? *Man on the right's blind. Black spectacles.* I know only two kinds of audiences, *Artur telling me as we left the stage, palm on my shoulder:* one coughing, the other not. This, unfortunately, was the former. *Then of course there are those who cram my mailbox with*—*Light gone nickelplated sunsmear. Existential Rottweilers can't remember who their owners are from one day to the next. Nickelplated sunsmear going, going, go*—*But the real question is how can Werner Heisenberg believe himself? Close your eyes. Open. Pick a spot in the sky and*—*Chilly birdsong. Mucky frogsong. Thank you, Edwin, for your redshift. Red hair. Hers. That woman over*—*How pale her*—*Teacher? Face like that actress. That's what losing faith feels like: memory of this afternoon falling. Edwin Hubble turning to me at dinner and asking:* Have you ever thought about how the history of astronomy is really the history of receding horizons? *Because you step out of your office at the university and there they are, the clods, shouting* Jew science! Jew science! *shouting* We're going to cut your throat, you kike scum! Artur, *I said,* Artur, tell me, please: What's the secret to playing like that? *and he answering without hesitation:* There's no secret, Einstein. I handle the notes no better than most. The art resides in handling the pauses between them. *And you looking up from your lectern and saying:* With what, your unfathomable imbecility? *Organ grinder cranking by the dock. Black frock coat. Leashed monkey. Miniature caravan wagon with cowboy wheels.* Pay the man to stop, please, *Artur would*—LEC-TURES AGAINST THE EINSTEIN HOAX, *the Working Committee of German Natural Philosophers billed it. What could I do except attend? Clap and bravo whenever they made a particularly idiotic point? Afterward the journalist asking.* The difference between stupidity and genius is that genius has its limits, *I told him. That's when cousin Elsa arranged for the bodyguard without letting me*—*Easy enough to*—*there: that man in the mackintosh even on sunny days, cigarette between his*—*Pretending to take in the organ grinder's slow pandemonium. Going. Going. Go*—*Darling cousin Elsa nakeding at the foot of our bed with a pistol in her hand.* Carry this, *she demanded.* But I don't know how to use it, *I said.* Learn, *she said.* Even *you* can do that, Albert. *Let the evening spread over you because there I stood as a boy in that doctor's office with my permanent sore throat.* Time for those tonsils to come out, *the tower of dreadful proclaimed. Mutti and Vati politely withdrawing. The tower frowning down. My stomach hurt. I had to pee.* Are you a brave German boy or a coward who cries because of a little pain? *I looked up at him, weighing my options. He swept me answerless off the floor and clumped me down on the chair.* Sit still, *he said. I sat still.* Open your mouth. *I opened my mouth. His long shears appeared from nowhere. They reached in and snipped out my tonsils before I—Lightning distended through the room. But I didn't cry. That's the—I sat there stifling a cyclone, thinking about my school, my teachers, how now they were inside me, too, among my teeth, among my—*

grammar : the clatter of time

The pale redheaded girl with swan's neck and freckles, Erika, the tall thin boy with wide shoulders and soft hands, Klaus, finishing their coffee and carrot cake with whipped cream and standing, first she, he following, to walk away from the bratwurst hut, from the small tables coveyed under a nearby oak, into the woods, hand in hand, some fairytale couple, organ grinder's music draining away behind them.

The pale redheaded girl in her school uniform, collarless, sleeveless black dress reaching her ankles, worn over white blouse, Erika, the tall thin boy with soft hands and loosened black tie, school jacket slung over left shoulder, Klaus, both lying to their parents about where they are today, at length stepping off the path to tunnel deeper into white birches streaked with black slashes until the bird fracas, squirrel fracas, leaves crackling beneath.

Erika thinking about the homework she must complete this weekend, the math problems, which she detests, the Latin, which she adores—especially the grammar of it, the Virgil, the language she someday wants to teach others to adore, how if you say it aloud you can hear melodies, the round sounds, the rolled r's, Klaus's fingers meshing with hers.

146

He less thinking than trying to open himself up completely to these next few minutes, knowing they won't come again, not like this, not in this order, intensity, the floral air, the dissipating sun, scents becoming tastes, Erika's touch the clatter of time, she and Klaus no longer moving, for either she stopped first or he stopped first or they both stopped together among those birches, his thoughts not caring whether he wants to think them or not, for Klaus has never kissed a girl before, for Erika's eyes are such a shiny light-hued blue they appear silver glass.

Erika recollecting as Klaus takes her other hand that other boy, the new one in school, tall and lean like him, swaggering up on her way home, she able to tell right away he was cocky and defenseless, a combination meaning part of her couldn't help falling for him while another couldn't help being revolted, he leaning in toward her as he passed, whispering close to her ear, *incredible eyes*, just like that, before continuing down the sidewalk as if nothing had happened.

Klaus remembering how last week he cut through the small park near school with friends and spotted Erika laughing among a group at a picnic table, he all at once wishing to sprint through the halls of a large villa looking for her, except he had already joined her, making small talk, hearing a former version of himself muster the courage to ask if she had ever been to Pfauen-insel, she saying no, he proposing casually maybe they should go sometime, and afterward, maybe, he proposing, a dance hall, Bühlers Ballhaus, do you know it?

Forsan et haec olim meminisse iuvabit, Erika recalling, she can't say why, lips touching lips, just like her lips touched that new boy's in the courtyard, line 203, Book One, after Aeneas's crew washed up on the shores of Carthage, she can't say why and then she can, *perhaps it will be pleasing to have remembered these things one day*, their lips touching, *iuvabit*, third-person singular future active indicative, his hand sliding down her side to her hip, up again, down, pressing his groin into hers, she with a jolt aware of that stiffness, because *I please, you please, we please*, because *that's how it is*, her friend Klara whispering to her as they lay side by side in bed at the sleepover last month, *that's how it is*, his hand sliding up to her left breast, cupping it, breath quickening, Klara explaining how boys want you to drown in affection just so they can paw you, that's why they listen, ask so many questions, smile at you with their voices, two weeks earlier her first period seeping forth in math class, brownish sticky stain in white undies, all that shame issuing from her body, Klara promising Erika and Erika promising Klara they would always remain best friends, exactly like this, although they will have forgotten each other's names in thirteen years, unable even to summon up each other's face, because there will have been too many other things to recall by then, because they will have both become afraid of all the time they still have to live through.

Maybe Pfaueninsel, Klaus proposing at that picnic table, because from that moment on he could look forward to seeing Erika again rather than looking back at having been with her, teeth unexpectedly clacking teeth, Erika giggling into his sour-milk-and-coffee mouth in surprise, both used to lying to their parents because their parents wanted to believe they had had children other than the children they had had, her giggle cutting short as his palm presses her breast through her white blouse and bra, reaches down to hike up her—

The pale redheaded girl in her school uniform giggling into his mouth and then not, his hands suddenly everywhere.

The tall thin boy, school jacket in a pile at his feet, leaving this earth.

His soft hands insistent, down to her ass, fondling, pressing his groin into hers, unaware in eighteen years on an afternoon not unlike this one he will find himself responsible for handcuffing young boys to their machine guns in central Berlin, no longer Klaus, wondering if he should kill himself before it's too late, wondering what kind of play everyone was putting on for him, untying the knot at the back of her dress, bending down briefly and lifting, without warning a finger between her thighs, his voice, the new one's in the courtyard—no—Klaus's, whispering close to her ear, the stale coffee and milk of it, the boyness.

The pale redheaded girl in her school uniform, Erika, pushing him back half an arm's length and in a single, determined gesture shoving her hand down the front of his trousers, closing her grip around him, unbuttoning with her other hand, then withdrawing in a scramble, little-girl *oh* rising from her throat.

Flummoxed, Klaus opening his eyes.

The pale redheaded girl's gaze focusing beyond him, over his shoulder, *there, through those trees—*

—and Klaus turning, scanning, fumbling to tuck in his shirt, scoop up his school jacket, *a man, a woman, they're watching us, small wicker basket of what in his hands, mushrooms big as turds, and the woman, dark frizzy hair, olive skin, engrossed, the man with the brushy mustache beside her, you can see it, they're spying on us, those goddamn Yids.*

walking radio static : twenty beautiful children

Leaning out the window of her hotel room in Lisbon thirteen years later, Hannah will recall the lurch in her chest as she caught sight of the girl's slim arm down the front of the boy's dark brown trousers. The look on her face as the girl became aware of them becoming aware of them over her boyfriend's shoulder.

Hannah and Martin were out collecting mushrooms in the Düppeler Forest and next thing they were voyeurs. Hannah wanted to step forward and apologize, mimic them, join them. Instead, she cupped Martin's elbow and quickly steered him back onto the path. He laughed all the way to the car, delighting in the unexpected encounter.

Martin's driver is waiting for them behind the wheel of a glassy black convertible with its top down. Humboldt University, busy wooing Martin, has provided both. Seeing the pair approach, the driver folds his newspaper, steps out, and opens the back door, expression that singular deferential German vacancy.

As the convertible crawls through Wannsee's town center, Hannah can't help it anymore and asks: How long do I have you for?

It never seems to occur to Martin to offer an answer before she inquires, yet he must know she will always inquire, even though he always seems genuinely startled when she does.

Sunday, he answers. And you?

Martin's hands are folded over his basket like a pregnant woman's over her belly. He has come up from Marburg to deliver a public lecture tomorrow. Hannah has come up from Heidelberg where she fled Martin by pursuing her doctorate under Karl Jaspers.

The problem is Martin has proved impossible to escape. Hannah and he can only stay apart so long—sometimes weeks, sometimes months—before one of them searches out the other in a fright of notes and letters.

(*Please kiss whatever part of you you can reach for me*, pens Martin. *P.S. Please stop writing me and try to be as happy as you can.*)

(*My first feeling about the rain was that it was like you*, pens Hannah. *Unavoidable.*)

And so they are together again, sitting in this chauffeur-driven convertible winding through Berlin's streets. The small wicker basket in Martin's lap holds six fat honeycombed morels. He will carry them back to Marburg's church bells in order to sauté them as a gift for his wife, their kitchen full of stories neither of them is telling.

Hannah refuses to attach a forename to that woman. She envisions her as human-shaped radio static moving from room to room in a deserted house on a gusty seacoast. Hannah removes the woman's two boys from the picture entirely.

She isn't quite twenty-one and Martin not quite thirty-eight and the thought flashes through her that she doesn't like his mustache's bristliness down there even though sometimes she does, very much.

Minced garlic sizzling in olive oil. Martin's delicate hands adding morel slices. Her own drastic non-presence burning through the scene. Hannah sees these things as she sees a row of parked bicycles expecting their owners outside the Wannsee Station.

They are on their way back to their hotel on Unter den Linden. There the student will have sex with her former professor, fantasizing about the boy and girl among the birches. The professor will shower with his former student, contemplating the diverse attributes of guilt, which neither of them feels.

Hannah hopes to catch a glimpse of either Greta Garbo or Thomas Mann somewhere among the enormous square marble columns in the lobby. Word has it both are overnighting among Hotel Adlon's grandeurs, she on her way home to Stockholm for a summer holiday, he on his way to Warsaw for a talk.

Not only does the Adlon boast both hot and cold running water, but also its own power plant, restaurant, ladies' lounge, library, music room, smoking room, barber shop, cigar shop, on-site laundry, several grand ballrooms, and an inner garden with Japanese-themed elephant fountain, gift from the Maharaja of Patiala himself, which will be mostly destroyed by a fire started in the wine cellar by drunken Red Army soldiers.

(What Hannah would give to shake Mann's hand and thank him for the pleasure of his syntax.)

It just occurred to me, she says, when you begin a sentence in German, you already have to know how it ends.

Naturally.

It's not like that in other languages. In English, in French, you live a sentence as you speak it. What does that say about us?

Do you believe the boy and girl back there were in love, schnucki? Martin asks. Was that love, do you think?

After the shower they will dress and return to Wannsee for the salon at the Arnhold Villa on the lake.

Hannah is working with Jaspers on a dissertation about the concept of love in St. Augustine. Martin's lecture will concern his first book. It has just appeared and he is tremendously relieved to get it out of him. Nobody in the audience will quite know what to make of what he will say. This idea pleases Martin immensely.

His Marburg colleagues warned him he was spending too many years on the thing. They told him privately it better be damn good. But their warnings couldn't rat their way in. What mattered to Martin was thinking. He continued to work at his own pace until he felt, not quite finished, precisely, but rather at least able to abandon the manuscript with something like a clear conscience. At the eleventh hour he turned in four hundred and thirty-eight pages entitled *Being and Time*. He is quietly confident it will change everything.

Different language structures lead you to different ways of being in the world, Hannah says. And, no, I believe they were in lust.

Good for them, says Martin, looking out at the city sliding past.

Hannah was eighteen when she began studying philosophy at university. Martin's name reached her like the rumor of a secret king. She signed up for his course on Plato's *Sophist*. On the first day of class the side door to the lecture hall opened and she was crazy for him. It wasn't something conscious, she will explain to an interviewer thirty years later in her office at Bard College. It took place, not in concepts, but in chemicals.

In Spanish, in Italian, Hannah points out, emotion and thought go hand in hand.

In German, you're saying, they're divorced.

I'm saying what does that mean.

It means our linguistic system evolved to moderate its users. Our language settles.

And our pair back there? They didn't seem very settled to me.

They weren't using German, schnucki. They were using their fingers and lips to talk with each other. This is sometimes referred to as having fun.

Martin introduced her to Hans Arnhold, the banker, and his wife, Ludmilla, twice. To Anna-Maria and Ellen Maria, their clever daughters, once. Hannah treasures her attendance at the salons. The Arnholds author a carefully selected anthology of artists, musicians, and intellectuals to do nothing but enjoy themselves. The forty-room main house overlooks a lawn sloping down to Lake Wannsee. The reception hall opens onto a spacious veranda that faces west. In warm weather people pour out to smoke cigars and watch the sunsets last forever.

Rolling beneath the Brandenburg Gate, they spot, in the park lined with trees and benches running up Unter den Linden's midriff, a man leading a bear on its hind legs at the end of a long chain secured to a wide leather belt around his waist. The man is playing a flute. Twenty beautiful children follow him as if in the opening to a folk tale.

Martin claps his hands in glee.

Hannah rejoices in Martin's pleasure, re-loves him, unable to imagine how it will be in another year or two, she then the wife of another man, when she will catch sight of Martin hurrying in the opposite direction through Berlin's mobbed central train station. Nearly brushing her shoulder, he will fail to recognize her. He will whisk by her as if by a stranger.

When I was a child, she will explain to that interviewer thirty years later, my mother once frightened me terribly. Do you know the story about the dwarf whose nose grows so long nobody knows him anymore? At the baker's once, she pretended I was that dwarf. I still remember the terror I felt as I cried: *But I'm your daughter, Mutti! I'm your Hannah! Don't you know me?*

That's what it felt like in that station. Devastated, I let Martin pass. Obviously I could have reached out. I could have caught his coat sleeve and his attention. But I didn't. What was the point? Everything we had done came thundering in.

Look! Martin shouts beside her. *Over there!*

eight words : a bike, a game, a new family moving

Rolling from beneath the Brandenburg Gate, Heinz spots a man leading a bear on its hind legs at the end of a long chain secured to a wide leather belt around the man's waist. He is playing a flute. Behind him trail twenty beautiful children.

White sleeves hiked, collars unbuttoned, Alwin and Heinz are heading back to the Schultheiss-Patzenhofer Brewery after a thirteen-hour workday triggered at five this morning when their alarm clocks became hysterical. Heinz and Alwin have delivered full-bellied wooden beer barrels and retrieved empties from bars, restaurants, and beer gardens as far away as Potsdam. The barrels are knolled six deep, four wide, and seven long in the back of their rattling old truck with a big advertisement for the brewery painted on its side, yellow and red on black.

All Heinz wants to do now is down his own stein and pork knuckle amid potato dumplings and cabbage with his buddies at the Ratskeller, go home and lunge into sleep beside his girlfriend, Christel, so he'll be ready to start the whole thing over again tomorrow.

When he was a kid, his life felt it was changing by the hour. There was always something unfamiliar coming at him. A bike he hadn't seen before. A game he hadn't played. A new family moving in next door, an old family moving out from the apartment above.

Then one day nothing changed anymore, always.

Since they met at the loading dock at five thirty, Heinz and Alwin have exchanged fewer than eight words. That's about their daily average. What's the point of wasting all that energy on sounds that never fit what you're trying to say?

And yet now Heinz feels he has something important to get off his chest.

Bear, he says.

What?

Alwin turns, back tight, muscles up and down his spine locked into two long iron bars, lets the scene sink in as their truck slows for curdling traffic.

Initially he assumes it's a man dressed in a bear suit, big head cocked osteoporotically forward, arms out straight, wrists curled down like a movie monster's. Except it isn't a man dressed in a bear suit. It's a bear. Once he saw one dance at the Zoological Garden. He was six. Seven. Six. His father slapped him on the back of the head when in his excitement he let some of his popcorn spill.

How about that, he says.

A minute, a minute and traffic opens. Heinz begins switching up through the gears. Their truck grinds past the Hotel Adlon, gaining speed.

Good work, he says, if you can get it.

Gotta learn to play the flute, Alwin says. Ain't worth it.

They both sense they may have just depleted their word allotment for the week, so they drop back into silence.

Heinz can't take his eyes off the bear, the man with the flute, those angel children, blond and straight-backed and regal. They aren't walking. They're marching. That's what they're doing. They're marching through the park with rigid little legs and rigid little arms and it's beyond words to witness.

The rattling old truck's roofed cab possesses neither windshield nor doors. Even above its motor Heinz can make out the tune the man is play-ing, although it isn't much, just three or four notes rippling up the scale, three or four notes rippling down, and—

Watch out! Alwin shouts.

Heinz's attention pivots back to the boulevard at the same instant the wet thunk arrives. He hits the brakes and slams forward into the steering wheel, bracing himself for the impact that has already taken place.

blacks

newsreel : four

Emelka Corporation

presents

—TODAY'S MOST THRILLING NEWS—

~ GERMANY IGNORES SOVIET-BRITISH RIFT ~

Our NOBEL LAUREATE *Gustav Stresemann*
in Baden-Baden parley
with Soviet Union's *Georgy Tchitcherin.*

Stresemann reaffirms German policy of
—ABSOLUTE NEUTRALITY—

Yet our Berlin Foreign Minister
says he continues to DEPLORE activities of the
COMMUNIST INTERNATIONAL.

Tchitcherin *insists* Russian

foreign policy is one of
—PEACE TOWARD ALL NATIONS—

Yet Stresemann warns
the **LEAGUE OF NATIONS** will *FAIL*
UNLESS ALL COUNTRIES DISARM;
urges Russia to join *NOW.*

~ ! **ECONOMY CONTINUES TO IMPROVE** ! ~

*Prussian Trade Minister's
Monthly Report Highly Favorable* !

BUILDING, TEXTILE, SHIP CONSTRUCTION
—*ALL UP*—

STEEL MILLS BOOKED THREE
MONTHS OUT !

The Berlin Stock Exchange Average
200 % ABOVE
this time one year ago !

—UNEMPLOYMENT *drops* by another *163,000*—
—WAGES for skilled labor *rise*—
—OPTIMISM *soars* across Europe—

—*! WE MUST BE DOING SOMETHING RIGHT !*—

lance olsen

~ DACHSHUND VILLAGE ~

Hang on to your seats—this is a LONG DOG *story*!

TIEFENBACH—a lovely village in
Lower Bavaria—
goes ALL OUT
for these sausage mutts—

And *WHY NOT*?
It says it gave BIRTH to the adorable breed
&
owes these pups its PROSPERITY!

They get away with MURDER
—RUNNING FREELY THROUGH THE STREETS—
—*visiting strangers' houses with impunity*—

—EVEN HELPING THEMSELVES TO LUNCH—
—AT THE LOCAL BUTCHER'S—

—*This is no place to be a cat*!—

IN TIEFENBACH DACHSHUNDS HAVE
REACHED THEIR GREATEST HEIGHTS—
OR SHALL WE SAY *LENGTHS*!

twenty-seven seconds ago : marigolds

It's like all the lights in the city splintered at once, Alfred Phillips has time to reflect before the gray voices swoop in around him like bats frantically collecting mosquitoes at twilight.

Twenty-seven seconds ago, Alfred halted between two cars parked in front of the Hotel Adlon.

He had told his pregnant wife, Eloise, he was on his way to the bakery across Unter den Linden and up Wilhelmstraße to fetch her a dozen of the best fruit, vegetable, and pig-shaped marzipans in Berlin. This was true. It was also true he was on his way to visit his lover, Marianne, whose flat sits two floors above the bakery.

Checking his pocket watch, Alfred stepped out from between those two parked cars and—

—and now he is starfished on the road, unsure whether those swooping gray voices exist inside his skull or out, his eyes are open or shut, his hands and feet still parts of him.

He is very sure, however, that the last thing he wants, the last thing he has ever wanted, is to make a public fuss. That isn't who Alfred Phillips is. Alfred Phillips is a cultivated twenty-nine-year-old unassumingly proud he has been fortunate enough to attend very good schools.

A diplomat who, once upon a time, believed he believed he wanted to be a writer. And then one morning he raised his head from his desk to discover he was on the team planning to meet with Gustav Stresemann sub rosa following the publicized Baden-Baden conference.

He has swum into his late twenties a devoted, kind, adoring husband with a palm-sized bald patch who, after that meeting, plans to spend Sunday sightseeing with Eloise.

Early Monday he will repair to London.

Early Tuesday he will repair to the embassy.

Early Monday he was supposed to repair to London.

Early Tuesday he was supposed to repair to the embassy.

It was Eloise, white hotel robe flapped open, belly mutinous with estuarial purple-brown stretch marks, firstborn due in a matter of weeks, asking him from the couch in their suite, where she has been trying to nap for the better part of the afternoon, heeding the doctor's instructions, if Alfred would be a dear and run over to that splendid little bakery, the what's it called, to pick up a dozen pieces of marzipan for her.

Alfred saw his opening and rose from the desk, where he had been reviewing notes for tomorrow's talks with the Stresemann team, slipped on his dark blue blazer, and said:

Of course, pet. Back in a jiff.

It was Alfred pulling closed his door in the Adlon and striding down the corridor, past a maid polishing the baseboard, contemplating how Marianne's opal skin, crow-black hair, and pink sheets smell like lemon oil, how surprisingly muscular her petite body is, how it dovetails with his own as if so designed, how she leans into him with such force when she embraces him at the threshold of her flat that Alfred has to take a euphoric step back with one foot to preserve his equilibrium.

Now it is this impossible light. It is hundreds of birds falling from the sky, hundreds of shuddering hearts, and the interior of a vast shadowy hangar wheeling with gray voices. It is this sensation that may or may not be other people's hands pressing against him, palpating, running up and down his arms and legs, which no longer seem to be his, the rant of traffic furiously lacking.

Herr Phillips, whispers Gustav Stresemann close to his ear, can you hear me?

Alfred knows it can't be Stresemann. Stresemann remained behind in Baden-Baden to luxuriate in the thermal baths. He isn't due back until late tonight.

Herr Phillips, Gustav Stresemann repeats, louder, can you hear me?

Yes, Alfred says.

Can you tell me where you are?

Alfred turns the question over.

No, he answers.

Good, says Stresemann. Then you're alive.

Marianne. Flori, too. Isabel goes without saying.

Alfred cherishes each of them.

Does he love Eloise?

They've always gotten along. They've always been there for each other. They met while students at Cambridge and bonded over the epiphany in their third year that, at the end of the day, they both lacked fire. At the end of the day, all they both honestly wanted to do was become harmless, content taxpayers.

Does he love Eloise?

Of course he does—beyond the power of language to occupy.

Does he hunger for Marianne, Flori, and Isabel?

Absolutely.

Things are as simple and baffling as that.

Each paramour provides Alfred with an essential piece of himself.

Marianne's firm, petite body in Berlin. Flori's fat, clumsy laughs in Paris. Isabel's briery, inflexible intelligence in Islington. Without them, Alfred couldn't be as thoroughly Alfred as he is.

Does he love Eloise?

Without Eloise's comradeship, maternal presence and social agility, tenderness and generosity and complacency, Alfred wouldn't be anything at all.

Alfred's mitochondria understand this.

His mitochondria understand Eloise's mitochondria understand this.

They have agreed without ever stooping to say so that certain alliances flourish by means of such accommodations.

The ambulance clang rises lazily out of those gray voices.

Alfred turns his attention in its direction to encounter himself recalling how grateful he was working with Stresemann's men in Baden-Baden. Stresemann himself was a model of diplomacy, decency, what his country has become since the war—a remarkable mixture of innate friendliness and beneficent pragmatism.

As Alfred waited beside his suitcase in the lobby for a taxi to the train station, Stresemann approached with extended hand and thanked him warmly for his efforts.

You know, he said, the courtesy that most becomes a victor has been denied Germany for a very long time. I'm glad to see it return in people like you, Herr Phillips.

Rumors began circulating in certain quarters that Germany had begun violating the Treaty of Versailles by testing military aircraft at southern airfields.

Tomorrow, confidentially, England's team will assure Germany's it believes no such thing.

Soviet distractions, it will say, and Stresemann will thank England for its clear-eyed appraisal.

Last year Germany was admitted to the League of Nations as a permanent member of the Security Council. It finally holds the power to veto resolutions. That means it can gain concessions from other countries on modifications to its borders, which, England believes, is only as it should be.

Once again Germany is taking its rightful place at the international table in order to keep the Bolsheviks at bay.

The splintered lights across the metropolis lickety-split reassemble behind Alfred's brow, flying together in spectacular reverse.

His eyes unclose by degrees.

Alfred expects to see the ambulance driver and his assistant perturbing around him, beyond them a circle of attentive onlookers.

He happens upon himself instead, standing among fifty or sixty people on the packed Adlon rooftop overlooking Berlin. One by one they are raising their faces to the first marigold traces threading the sky.

An undernourished woman beside him with outlandish red hair wears a man's tuxedo and bowtie. She has applied so much powder to her angular face she reminds Alfred of one of those blind fish that live in caves. She snorts up the white string of cocaine on the back of her raised hand, licks the leftovers, becomes conscious of Alfred watching her.

Care for a line, darling? she asks. Extraordinary shit.

Stresemann told me I was alive, says Alfred.

What a joker.

Alfred reviews her.

Listen, darling, she says. We're all already dead. Some of us know it. Some of us don't. The baby you and your wife were expecting, to cite a case in point.

Our baby?

Your wife's labor pains are starting…let me see…just about now. Things won't go well, I'm afraid. Would you like to shimmy?

What are you talking about?

All you have to do is relax and rely on your shoulders. Tell me what it smells like.

The dance?

1927.

I don't know. Rosewood. Wetted ashes.

Wrong, darling. It smells like tomorrow. Come. Dance with me.

The undernourished woman raises her arms to her sides like a tuxedoed scarecrow and lets her head fall back, beaming at the show above.

wish images : asja, architectonics

1. *The only way of honestly knowing a person is to love him or her without hope,* Walter Benjamin pencils in his notebook, hunched on a dark green bench in the dark green shade of a linden.

A bear occurs, a man playing a flute followed by twenty otherworldly children.

2. Walter crosses out the sentence. He has spent his entire day here, the last three, in combat with a three-page essay about Parisian arcades for the *Frankfurter Zeitung.* The essay refuses to stay in its skin. It keeps wanting to unfurl into something larger, messier, less itself.

3. *Suppose I were to begin by recounting,* he pencils in his notebook, *how many cities have revealed themselves to me in my expeditions for books. Suppose I were to speak of a time, ours, when even the best*

readers have become frightened of imperfect, torrential monographs—ones that fan out into dangerous mazes.

Suppose I were to bring up how easy a certain kind of completeness is.

4. He scratches out that paragraph, writes in his choked scribble *I am falling in love with lostness*, then come the brakes, that woman's shriek.

5. When he raises his head everything already exists in another tense.

6. An old truck, advertisement for a brewery across its side, has run up onto the curb in front of the Adlon. Several empty barrels have burst on the sidewalk. A smartly dressed man is splayed in the street, pedestrians vectoring in.

7. (*When a world war breaks out, all you can do is begin to translate the works of Baudelaire as faithfully as possible.*)

8. The bear man stops. His triad of notes. The twenty otherworldly children stop, at first confused about where to look.

One points, a perfect girl, mouth opening, nickel-blue eyes wide with the world.

9. Walter squints through his chunky spectacles to determine if the man is alive or the other thing.

10. Suppose, he considers, his weak heart twinging, I am falling in love with disjunction. Medieval alleys full of flowers. Suppose I am falling in love with learning to interrupt my—

11. Three years ago. Capri. Ernst Bloch crumpled down the newspaper he had been reading and glared at Walter over its dried-seagull remains. The pair reclined in chaise longues on their pension's balcony amid a tumble of shiny white houses overlooking the Bay of Naples.

How absurd it must seem, Bloch proclaimed, for an immortal soul destined for heaven or hell to find itself sitting in the kitchen in the form of a maid.

12. The bear waiting for orders.

13. The children.

14. *We may call these images wish images; in them the collective seeks—*

15. But most of all the tiny squares. Medieval alleys full of bougainvillea clinging to stone walls. Plumbago. Yellow, red, powder blue rowboats pulled up on the Marina Grande's pebbly beach. And Bloch saying: The most tragic form of loss isn't the loss of security. It is the loss of the capacity to imagine things other than they are.

16. For you were born under the sign of Saturn, planet of detours and delays, blunders and stubbornness; of those who see themselves as books, thinking as a method of gathering, organizing, yet always knowing when to stray, when to wander off.

17. *For to lose your way in a city or a person requires a great amount of willpower.*

18. It is Bloch proclaiming from his chaise longue, newspaper seagull crumpled in his lap, and emaciated Rilke all those years after that first meeting at the University of Munich, praising in a letter to Walter from somewhere among the Swiss Alps Mussolini's New Year's Eve speech.

What soaring language! What lustrous discourse! Fascism, our great healing agent!

19. The hotel doormen holding onto the driver of the truck until the police show up, and the belief Jewishness means a promise to further European culture, each epoch dreaming the one to follow.

20. Inaccurately.

21. These moments, those hours, the other days: Had Walter really accomplished anything at all?

Wonders Walter.

22. It is Baudelaire jotting on a scrap of paper *Sois toujours poète, même en prose*— *Always be a poet, even in prose*—and the ambulance disturbance rising on the far side of the heavy, coal-smoked Brandenburg Gate, and the found object, the readymade, the already extant message, the chance encounter, the transitory, the fugitive, the contingent, that half of art of which the other half is eternal and immutable.

23. There was the juncture at which he understood he was not to become an academic instructor.

There was that injury.

24. Wine. Bread. Thickly sliced salami.

25. A lizard with azure scales panting rapidly on a fence rail.

26. The sun, a glossy orange in the sunset sky: Capri.

27. There was that juncture, and there will be the one in which he can no longer remember what he wants as he reaches languidly for the bottle of tablets on his hotel nightstand in room number three.

28. Yet now it is just those days with Bloch on that balcony, the nights with Asja Lācis in her bed, long umber hair tousled.

Naked.

Yawning.

Her unselfconscious stretching, her body Y-ing on the mattress.

Walter was completely open about the Latvian Bolshevik theater director when his wife, Dora, asked in her letters.

But only when she asked.

(She asked just once.)

29. *Writing about a given place at a given time puts its existence between quotation marks, plucks it from its native context by engendering unanticipated new ones.*

This is collage's capacity, through cutting up and cutting off, to open up and ou—

30. I don't believe we will be getting married, *mana saulīte*. I find divorce too hard on the nerves.

Asja footnoting in mid-stretch.

31. Dora remaining behind in Berlin with their nine-year-old son, anxious Stefan, and Asja introducing Walter over dinner to Marxism as historical mutiny and over late night Prosecco to sex as cellular whirlwind.

32. Writing that looks like writing, thinking that looks like thinking, has come to feel to Walter progressively faded and fated.

Suppose, he pencils in his notebook, *I were to rethink everything.*

Suppose I were to start all over again.

33. Thirteen years later, twenty-some-odd changes of address behind him, standing outside the Bibliothèque Nationale on a thick spring day, twenty-four hours before the Germans howl into Paris with orders to arrest that Jew intellectual, Walter hands over his color-coded notes—green language, yellow, red; diagrams; copies of images that have collared his curiosity—to his grouper-mouthed librarian friend Georges Bataille.

34. Asja's double enlivening: the erotic and the political slurred into a single unfathomableness.

35. Or this man, weak heart, weakening lungs, a mobile intelligence unit moving through the metropolitan streets, he likes to imagine himself as, although what would happen if you began to consider the essay you are composing, not as a—

36. After this crapulent war, Georges telling Walter outside the library on that balmy pre-invasion day, Europe will resemble a Sade novel. Watch out for Duc de Blangis. He will be everywhere.

Georges not grinning, but rather turning away, returning to work.

Walter watching his friend's lightly pigeon-toed gait.

37. *Suppose you began to regard the essay you are writing not as a piece of music that must move from first note to last, but rather as a building you could approach from various sides, navigate along various paths, one in which perspective continually changes.*

This building, we might submit, would constitute a literary architectonics that pits itself against narrative's seemingly inflexible arc from birth to curtains.

38. These lines written by the man who earned his Ph.D. cum laude eight years ago with a dissertation on art criticism in German Romanticism, yet who has been assiduously unable to find academic employment ever since.

That injury, too.

39. (Among others.)

40. There is that brief deliberation over emigrating from Germany to Palestine and how the bottle of morphine tablets catches the caramel sun in tiny room three at the Hotel de Francia on the Catalonian coast one autumn afternoon in 1940, police guard posted outside Walter's door demurely clearing his conscience every now and then.

41. Written by the thirty-four-year-old journalist unable to support himself, let alone his family, through his own labor, and

so forced for a time to ask his wife to stop loving him so he could return to Berlin to reside with his parents.

42. *To reside with his—*

43. *Ne cherchez plus mon coeur; les bêtes l'ont mangé.*
Baudelaire jotting on a scrap.

44. There is that slightly less brief deliberation over emigrating to the United States through neutral Portugal as the Germans howled closer, and how Max Horkheimer negotiates a travel visa for Walter, who will only be able to flee over the Pyrenees as far as Spain before the Franco regime cancels all transit permits and orders the authorities to return those carrying them to France.

45. And on 25 September, 1940, there is that Spanish official with the pinched lips telling the group of Jewish refugees Walter has joined to prepare for deportation the following morning, the emptiness on Hannah Arendt's face taking in this information, on her husband the poet and philosopher Heinrich Blücher's, on their friend the Hungarian novelist Arthur Koestler's, on the German photographer Henny Gurland's, and her son Joseph's.

46. Yet, despite the future, the bear man steps into motion again, his melody rediscovering itself.

47. One by one, the otherworldly children.

48. *Do not look for my heart anymore; the beasts have eaten it*, jotting the poet who spent his last two years between Brussels and Paris, semi-paralyzed and unable to speak after a massive stroke.

49. The emptiness on the ambulance driver's face as he employs a plain white sheet to cover the bodily fluids held in by tender skin.

50. Or the emptiness on the doctor's face during each of his four visits to tiny room three through that September afternoon and evening, administering injections and bloodletting, as if these things might in the end somehow alter the configuration of spacetime.

51. It is the ambulance driver's face, even at this distance, and Asja's body in her bed, sheetless in silvery sun, along with the belief writing as collage draws attention to the sensuality of the page even as it strips itself of the tedious, tendentious pretense of originality.

Suppose, therefore, it could be argued—

52. *Suppose we were to call it a meditative practice that allows one to be surprised by what one says next.*

A practice, we could even submit, of reading.

53. Or the other manuscript, completed, which Walter will carry in his suitcase from Paris to Portbou, which will disappear forever.

54. *Suppose, therefore, it could be argued that we are all collage artists,* pencils Walter, then crosses out the sentence, for there will be that juncture in two years at which Dora and he will have become separated, then divorced, that juncture in thirteen at which the other Jews in his refugee party for no discernible reason will be allowed sudden passage through Spain into Portugal.

55. Four days later all will safely reach Lisbon.

56. Minus one.

57. It is the ambulance driver's empty face, even at this distance, and Hannah Arendt admiring the terracotta rooftops, the pale yellow dwellings, bunching down the steep Lisbon hillsides into bluegreen seasprawl.

58. The Spanish police will refer to the deceased forty-eight-year-old in their correspondence with Max Horkheimer, who will query about the details of his friend's passing, as *that German gentleman*.

59. *That German gentleman about whom you inquire*, the Spanish police will state, *died of heart failure*.

60. *Cerebral hemorrhage*, the medical certificate will state.

61. The town judge listing Walter's possessions at the time of death: *suitcase leather, gold watch, pipe, passport issued in Marseilles by the American Foreign Service, six passport photos, an X-ray, one pair of spectacles, various magazines, a number of letters, a few papers, contents unknown, and some money.*

62. *A few papers, contents un—*

63. How, because of confusion surrounding his identity, Walter will be buried in leased-niche number 563 in the Catholic section of the Portbou cemetery. When no one remembers to keep up payments, his remains will be quietly exhumed and moved in the summer of 1945 to the town's common burial ground, where their exact location will over time become unrecalled.

64. Four days after Walter reaches for the bottle of morphine tablets he brought with him from Marseilles, just in case, Hannah Arendt will lean out the window of her Lisbon hotel room, relishing the act of breathing, recollecting that young couple she and Martin once stumbled across in the Düppeler Forest, while admiring the terracotta rooftops and pale yellow dwellings bunching down the steep hillsides.

65. Below, the streetcars clanking by.

66. Bumblebee scooters revving.

67. That greasy scent of reprieve billowing up around her a flash before she turns and steps back into her life.

what happens next : gorgeous failures

But what happens next? Greta Garbo asks Emil Jannings.

She is leaning out the window of her suite at the Adlon, speaking to him over her shoulder, absorbed by the chaos in the street below.

Traffic has come to a standstill. Fitful horns leap above the throb of motor engines like a pulse irregularly drumming. A beer truck has hit someone. It must have been just a minute or two before she stepped over to this very spot and pulled back these thick drapes and opened this window wide to see.

The ambulance driver and his assistant are sliding the stretcher on which lies a sheeted body into the back of their top-heavy—

Guess, says Emil from the opulent chair with gold trim by the fireplace. His legs are crossed like a woman's, his swollen white hands balled in his lap like two blind invertebrates. What do you *think* happens next?

Greta thinks, she does, but not about that.

Rather, she thinks about how she will always remember the illustrious Emil Jannings' prim red bowtie blooming from his prim white shirt collar, his prim brown suit, so completely at odds with what appear to be congenitally ghoulish yellow bruises ringing his eyes.

I couldn't begin to, she says, straightening, turning.

He's a cashier. I'm a cashier. At a bank. His boss asks me to carry a grand in securities from Milwaukee to Chicago. On the train I meet a blond bombshell. Phyllis Haver. Do you know her? You should see that woman in sequins. She flirts and gets him, gets me, to buy her a bottle of champagne. They end up at a bar. We end up in a bed. And next morning he wakes—

Beside her in a swank hotel room?

Emil stages a soundless laugh, makes an applause gesture without bringing his hands fully into contact with each other.

Alone in a dive, he says. Sans securities.

Turning to face him, leaning back against the windowsill, she lifts her cigarette, lets smoke smart out her nostrils. Greta would prefer to look at what is going on down there, behind her, grim as it might be, because that is how it comes at you, isn't it, and go to bed early and make the next two days pass as uneventfully as possible, drinking fancy cocktails by the elephant fountain in the inner garden before continuing her trip north to visit her family.

Guess, says Emil from across the ocean. Go on. Take a shot.

Greta adored her older sister, Alva, daddy's little girl—*Lillan* they called her, Little One.

At twenty-two Lillan hurriedly died of lymphatic cancer while Greta filmed in the States. Near the end the family moved Lillan into a sanatorium in Södermalm, from which she stopped writing Greta her weekly balloons of encouragement and love.

On Greta's way to the lot one morning a gofer panted up beside her and handed her a telegram: *A döende komma hom far. A dying come home father.* Except Louis B. Mayer wouldn't let Greta come home, refused to let her leave the set to be with Lillan, went so far as to have the MGM lawyers write up a threatening letter Greta couldn't fully parse, even though she parsed it completely.

Do you have any *idea* what that crap would cost me, kiddo? Louis boomed at her from his jumbo white desk in his jumbo white office. Forget about it.

What color are her eyes? Greta hears herself asking, traffic an angry panic behind her.

Heart-stopping green, says Emil. Even in a room packed with people, the camera always picks out Phyllis. Approaching her, you feel yourself becoming less significant. So August Schilling—me—hunts down the hussy, pleads with her for the money. When that doesn't work, he tries to bully her—at which point her accomplice raps on the door, Schilling answers, and *wham*: the big goon knocks him cold and drags him to some nearby railroad tracks.

Without anybody noticing?

Narrative hocus-pocus.

She closes her eyes, shivers at how fast it comes at you, the poor man in the street, opens them as if these minutes were merely these minutes, and recites: *Anyone who doesn't love Hollywood is either crazy or sober.* Who said that?

Greta pictures a perfectly average man stepping off the curb, contemplating what, what was he contemplating, and next old ladies with dark parasols mushroomed; everyone looking on, passersby, the doormen, that couple with a pram, a boy springing off his fat bicycle. How could such a thing—it whirls in at you full tilt, doesn't it, a witch in tattered rags. That's what Lillan must have—

And then the traffic accumulating. The restless horns. The onlookers. This gradual drawing-together of everything into one incomprehensible center, everything briefly connected to everything el—

I rouse in mid-strip, Emil is saying. A perhaps not wholly unsurprising struggle ensues. Punches are thrown. Wrestling abounds. I somehow manage to throw the big goon under a train speeding by at the right moment. The police believe the mangled body is mine. I'm dead. Twenty years pass. We find our protagonist worn down, worn away, become a white-bearded trash collector in a cemetery. And who do you suppose he catches sight of one day on rounds?

Greta raises and lowers her shoulders.

My own family placing a wreath on his grave. It's Christmas. Snow-storm. Suddenly Schilling's selling cigarettes from a box round his neck on a street corner. Glancing up, I notice my name in lights on a marquee across the way. Only it's my son's, August Schilling Junior. I taught him to play violin when he was a kid. While I've been away, he's developed into a big musician. Tonight he's giving a concert. I go in, and, from the nosebleeds, I watch. Junior concludes his set by announcing he'll play a cradlesong his papa used to play him.

And the credits roll?

After one final shot: Me walking away, carrying in my pocket a dollar my son gave me, August gave August, not recognizing the broken bum is his undead dad.

Is it possible, Greta wonders, it wasn't an accident at all? What if he stepped into the street deliberately? There's always that possibility. The truck leaping at him from the left. Down flying the sky. Up flying the boulevard. What if what he did were an act, not of carelessness, but defiance—*I can do this and you can't stop me*? And there he lies, hearing how everybody else persists in living around him. That's how it must come at you: your last awareness the sounds of the world starting to go on without you.

That's what loneliness must feel like in its purest form: the closeness of people, touches, tastes deserting you.

I said: *You know something?* Emil repeats.

I was just thinking—Wouldn't life be wonderful if we only knew what to do with it?

Emil stages another soundless laugh and clap, says: You should get married, Fraulein Garbo. You'd make some American lawyer very happy. Will you look at the time? I must be on my—

With that he rises creakily, bows, reaches out both hands to clasp one of hers, lifts it to his mouth, the prim actor in the prim red bowtie bidding adieu, and, as his lips touch her skin, he sees briefly into the conditional /

that exact moment five months from now Greta forgets about this meeting / the noun of his name draining of substance / that moment in fourteen she raises her head in Louis' jumbo white office / listening to him berate her new film / *The Two-Faced Woman* / pronouncing it a complete flop / and she barely thirty-five / in the end there will be no lawyer / no marriage / no children / no more interviews or appearances / *a form* the newspapers postulating *of giving up* / *sure* she says / *maybe* she believes / in twenty-four years when she raises her hand to take the Oath of Allegiance / citizen of a country which will always feel like somebody else's / you do what you have to do to get by / father's lesson / those malevolent stoves in that fairytale / the blind masses shoveling in their burning hearts / which flare into flame / then belch back as black smoke that keeps them blind / and the rest of her life a wandering from room to room in her flat / peering down on 52nd Street / all that grime and neon / Jimmy Ryan's Bar / 3 Deuces / her closest friends / *like sisters* she says / her cook and housekeeper / those aimless walks through Manhattan / Paris / London / Vienna / frumpily dressed / like some bag lady / huge sunglasses beneath huge droopy brimmed hats / stopping to browse antique shops / not because of the tchotchkes / but because people leave you in peace there / her name shapeshifting over time / Greta to Miss G. / Miss G. to Miss Harriet Brown / Miss Harriet Brown to Miss Karin Lund to Miss Klown / yes / hotel registers / restaurant bills / Chinese laundry / never fooling anybody naturally / perhaps not even herself / and then her doctor reports across his desk matter-of-factly *breast cancer* / *go to hell* she responding without a pause / somehow even then knowing his words won't kill her / it will be something else / slow periodontal corruption / gastronomical rot / kidney failure / dialysis six hours three times a week / that lazy wrecking of Miss Klown / followed by her final wish / *burn this body then get it home* / ashes interred in Skogskyrkogården / simple reddish tombstone / almost exactly sixty-three years from this very kiss / the one Emil bestows upon her before straightening, smiling into her eyes with newfound tenderness, believing Greta's eyes might even be smiling back (although he is wrong), and gently releasing her soft young hand to take his leave.

And as his lips touch her skin Greta sees briefly into the conditional / the exact moment in two years Emil reaches out both hands to introduce himself to Marlene Dietrich / his new co-star in that movie he is making / *The Blue Angel* / redo of the hammy novel by Thomas Mann's banal brother Heinrich / Emil unimpressed by Dietrich's looks / what he's seen of her acting / both hausfrau chunky / and from the start they argue fiercely about politics on their breaks / in the days when politics didn't matter / and the moment in six years when the joke goes out of it / Marlene telling him *fuck off you piece-of-Nazi-shit* / *I'm moving to America* / he responding *you know what you are my dear?* / *you're a nasty little pig of a traitor* / *plus you pencil in your eyebrows too thin* / because Emil is loyal / the Führer won the election for God's sake / give the man a chance / God knows *someone* needed to take charge / the moment in nine Reich Minister Goebbels reaches out to shake Emil's hand / naming him Artist of the State / waves of humility washing over him / *a great patriot* Goebbels calls him / and in the end there coming not one marriage / no / but three / film actresses / gorgeous failures / just like the war itself / which commences so well / yet somehow two years on everything falling apart / the disbelief of it in the faces you pass on the streets / how could Stalingrad—/ the sour fortitude in the pedestrians' eyes / the bombs beginning / your last movie / *Where is Mr. Belling* / aborted in mid-shoot / and afterward you stumbling through the ruins that were your capital / the Allies raping our women / stealing our food / shooting civilians in the squares / *target practice* the Soviets call it / and Emil carrying his Oscar statuette through the smashed lanes / showing it to every soldier he met / proof of his ties with Hollywood / *the good guys loved me* / except the Ivans don't give a shit / *denazification* they say / the rest of his life turning into his punishment / and the moment in twenty Emil raises his hand to become an Austrian citizen / last country on Earth to welcome him / allow him to retire quietly into a quaint village on the shores of Lake Wolfgang / glacier-green as Phyllis Haver's eyes / and that moment in twenty-three his doctor reports matter-of-factly across his desk *liver cancer* / *go to hell* he responding without a pause / somehow even then knowing the man's words won't kill him / it will be something else / except they do kill him / leisurely

/ with more pain than he knew one human being could endure / months and months of it / another minute / another minute / another minute / until five had collected / then fifteen / half an hour / only to start all over again / stomach packed with glass shards / morphine pointless / agonizing turds coming out white as chalk / flesh orange / in the end nothing save a great pounding in the middle of a bed / bitter January night / almost exactly twenty-three from this very kiss / the one he bestows upon Greta before straightening, smiling into her eyes with newfound tenderness, and gently releasing her soft young hand to take his leave, once again turning into a stranger.

breeding + transmission : the lives so beautiful, so red

But what happens next? wonders one of the doormen at the Adlon, smiling at Thomas Mann who, without noticing him, enters the lobby through the door he is holding open.

The ambulance driver eases down the gas pedal, this thought straying through his consciousness: *Thank God for cheap tobacco.*

In a mangy café tucked up a nearby alley Bertolt Brecht takes another bite of carrot cake and jots down on his napkin an idea that has just struck him: *One can view people as a peculiar byproduct stories use for breeding + transmission.*

At the table behind him, a
student with a mossy five-day
growth of beard takes a sip of
coffee and turns a page in *Passionate Journey*, Frans Masereel's
wordless novel in woodcuts,
remembering how, when asked
once by an interviewer, Thomas
Mann mischievously named
it his favorite film—and then
mouthing the words: *What a
putz.*

So that was death, the boy with the grimy face under the
frayed tweed cap concludes, peddling his fat bike past the
café in which Brecht and the student sit, tasting factory
smoke and automobile exhaust on his tongue. *I have just
seen a man die. I have just seen that. That means he can
never be alive again. That means I wonder what mama's
making for dinner. Beets. I bet it's beet soup.*

A few meters behind the boy walks a
couple with a pram, the young wife
asking her husband without speaking:
*Do you remember how you stood me to
pig knuckles and beer that night?*

The husband asking himself:
*Are those people up there on the
roof? What in the world are they
doing?*

It must be time, realizes Alfred Phillips' wife Eloise, first
cramps spiking through her abdomen as she tries rising
from the sofa, the suite tumbling cockeyed, she losing
her footing, falling back, missing the cushions, her white
hotel robe flapping open, her body without warning
spread-eagle on the rug between couch and coffee table,
lump of brownish mucus oozing from between her legs,
*the phone is where is the doctor not in this lousy swamp just
a couple marzipan just—*

Outside her door a maid pol-
ishes the baseboard running the
length of the third-floor hall,
reckoning as she works: *This wax
better last longer than that shite
before or it'll be me here on my
aching knees again next week, too,
it will.*

—little tail all gray and purple hanging there no longer than my pinkie touch it Rolf said go ahead it won't bite you, a teenage girl passing three old ladies in the park that runs up the middle of Unter den Linden recounting, *and that's what all the fuss is about that's it really you've got to be kidding me—*

A mathematics professor, for whose career his colleagues once held out greater hope, waits for the ambulance to pass, then steps off the curb, over a cat's soggy corpse in the gutter, on his way to his office at Humboldt University, the dream he had last night briefly surfacing: *I was swimming through waves made of numbers, a vast sea of primes, they were so soft, like a tiger's belly, and the fives so beautiful, so red.*

The first snow every year, realizes the plum-cheeked gypsy woman, legs cut off at the pelvis, set out this morning by her son like a bust at the foot of the wall two meters behind Ernst Toller to sell mismatched shoelaces on a towel spread before her—*it is like waking up in a foreign country, like this one, yours but not, like seeing everything for the last time, air sweet and cool, cool but never really cold, oiliness gone out of it, the soot, sky a sheet of luminous white silk, all rules lost, the logic of it, edges, and—*

—*and thirty marks she whined thirty marks in that way she has,* the salesman goes off without warning on his after-work stroll to the Kupfergraben tram, *and what do we have to show for it but a couple shelves to flaunt her stupid ceramic elves thirty marks God in Heaven.*

Staring over at her flat's door from the kitchen table two floors above the bakery on Wilhelmstraße, Marianne waits patiently for Alfred Phillips to arrive, the question barely beginning to uncoil inside her: *Do you think maybe it slipped his—*

radical faith : the minutes in which you are sitting are on fire

—Friday, the journalist types, Kurt Severing types, sitting at his kitchen table one floor above the kitchen table at which Marianne waits patiently for Alfred, who won't arrive. I am typing It's Friday instead of writing the book review whose deadline is, what, three hours away now. Two. 8:30. Otherwise it won't get into Sunday's paper, he types, I won't get paid, and sometimes filling the page with language feels like you're getting somewhere, like it's enough. Steppenwolf. Strange title. Reality within. Despair the gateway to transcendence. Hesse's latest exaggerations. As if politics were a minor inconvenience to the psyche, something you could will out of your life. Easy enough belief to buy into, so long as you live in a nice neighborhood and forget you have a body, a history, a culture, a brain, a soul big enough to consider somebody besides yourself. And yet you can't escape the threat of all this disturbing whiteness in front of you, he types, Kurt Severing types, intensely conscious his room has become a nervous portal to other—how can he explain it?—to other ranges. Kurt can sense the electrostatic currents streaming around him. He knows that sounds crazy. He knows the problem with introspection is that it's bottomless. When did he first notice? Four years ago he walked down to the bakery for breakfast and heard the newsboy on the corner announcing that that petty agitator Hitler had killed himself after a failed coup attempt in some Munich beer hall. Shot himself through the heart before the police could arrest him. Only the next time Kurt left his room he found the street below exactly as it had always been. Von Hindenburg still president. Wilhelm Marx still chancellor. The trams on schedule. Occasionally realities entangled. You couldn't help picking up on it. Sometimes the headlines are unrecognizable, packed with names, places, circumstances he knows nothing about. His friends on the other side—they possess the same names, faces, and habits as his friends on this side—they've begun worrying about him. They read his growing befuddlement, his inability to recall easy words and occurrences, as first signs of a rattletrap memory. Entering the newspaper office frightens him. He can see his editor's eyes altering when Kurt speaks up at meetings. Or maybe he has read one too many novels. He wants to get up from his desk and go to the café and meet a friend, any friend—preferably a woman friend; a woman might understand better than a man what he is trying to say—to whom he can confess that he has finally read one too many novels. Not, Kurt would explain, Kurt types, because he doesn't like novels. He does. Kurt does. More than anything. But each keeps proving something Kurt always intuited: novels make precisely nothing different. Forever. He doesn't want to think about it. He can't stop thinking about it. You can appreciate the radical faith each embraces, even the most faithless. Still, their rhythms, syntax, metaphorical alchemy, every sentence an act of awareness, their desperate expressions of possibility (which are always desperate expressions of light), possess the extraordinary power to change nobody. Medicine. Matters of state. Automobiles. What color shirt you put on this morning. These make things other than they were. But novels—imagine all the ones that have been published. Imagine all the humans that have read them, are reading them, will read them, yet stubbornly continue behaving just like humans. Imagine all the societies that ponder them, teach them, write about them, talk about them, reverently pass them down from generation to generation, pretend to care, yet stubbornly continue behaving just like societies. People carry on killing, brutalizing, bullying, cheating, swindling, stealing, lying, gambling, overeating, fretting, celebrating selfishness, messiness, laziness, neuroses, arrogance, rudeness, despotism, greed, hypocrisy, impatience, vengefulness, manipulation, disloyalty, mercilessness, pessimism, childish dependence—and there novels are, supposing they act as queries designed to bring about contemplation, commiseration, provocation, transformation, when all they accomplish is to confirm that everything is made to be broken. And so consider the consequence of their presence in our lives. There is none. I want that cup of coffee. There is none. I want novels that know they can't do anything and yet try to do it anyway. There aren't any. I want to ask my café friend: Is anyone still honestly interested in stories? She might respond: That's an easy one: everyone and no one. The very idea of her reply is exhausting. Or she might ask me in return: What do you mean by stories? She might point out: We can't even talk about the question because The Notebooks of Malte Laurids Brigge exists, you idiot. And you've seen those excerpts from what Robert Musil is working on, those bits from Alfred Döblin's montage thing, Kurt types, raising his head while typing "Kurt types, raising his head while typing 'Kurt types, raising his head while typing'" to see the minutes in which he is sitting are on fire, typing "to see the minutes in which he is sitting are on fire, 'typing "to see the minutes in which he is sitting are on fire"'" because it is clear to him—what is clear to him?—it is clear to him—clear to Kurt Severing—

i spoke to her as a woman : she answered me as a man

hannah höch inadvertently completes kurt severing's thought
—*Berlin is a Dadaist photomontage*, she scrawls in the margins of her sketch-book, sitting on a crate in the storeroom at the back of a small gallery in Wedding, here from the Netherlands for a week to help set up her new show (the *vernissage* in half an hour), sleeping on a cot by night, by day helping repaint the walls, *all nonsense, travesty, incongruity, shock, noisy ephemeral machines that whir and clank but fail to accomplish a thing, instantaneous art that isn't pretty, proclaiming: Your belief in reason and progress did this, got us to this point, your bourgeois metaphysics, and we are here to end it.*

a brief history of the previous sentence
You were born thirty-eight years ago—not Hannah, but Anna: Anna Therese Johanne Höch—in Gotha, Thuringia, very near the precise geographic center of Germany, its pith, its crux, an area with almost noth-ing to recommend it, your parents removing you from school when you were fifteen to care for your youngest sister, but you sneaking back eight years later to study glass design and graphic arts in Berlin, your father hav-ing forbidden you to consider the various uselessnesses called painting and sculpture.

zurich café: version one

One evening in 1916 at the Cabaret Voltaire, Tristan Tzara picking up the French-German dictionary lying on the table next to his beer, opening it, and stabbing a random page with his letter opener.

The word the letter opener chooses is French babytalk for *hobbyhorse*.

In Romanian it means *yes yes*.

In German, *get off my back*.

wish image : a.

I would like to show the world today as an ant sees it, Hannah scrawling in the storeroom, *and tomorrow as the moon sees it,* wondering about all the things she might mean by that—in the middle of it the door opening, the gallery owner slipping in his head to say:

It's time, Frau Höch. Shall we go?

hand over woman's head

When I was six, I told my father I wanted to be an artist when I grew up. He looked down at me for a long time and then replied flatly: You can't do both, Anna.

a brief history of the previous sentence

In 1915 enrolling in a graphics class at the National Institute of the Museum of Arts and Crafts and falling in lust with Raoul Hausmann, that wide-mouthed, fat-egoed, monocle-wearing Austrian artist-writer-sound-poet and cofounder of the Berlin Dada circle.

Raoul's brain and cock, you coming to believe, the transcendental incarnate.

Moving to the capital to be with him, landing a job in the handicrafts department for The Ullstein Press, designing dress and embroidery patterns for two of its magazines.

The Lady.

The Practical Berlin Woman.

three phrases from tzara's manifesto

1. I am against manifestoes.

2. Journalist virgins.

3. *Boomboom, boomboom, boomboom.*

wish image : b.

Photomontage embodied our refusal to play the part of the artist, Hausmann explaining to an interviewer, already using the past tense. (It is 1927. It is an upscale restaurant off Savignyplatz, lunch courtesy of the interviewer's newspaper. The first automatic record changer has been introduced, the first Volvo just premiered in Gothenburg. Bavaria has just lifted its ban on Hitler's speeches, Henry Ford just announced the production of the last Model T.) *We regarded ourselves as engineers, and our work as construction: we assembled our work, like a fitter.*

the practical berlin woman

We are delighted to report a truly contemporary breed of female has appeared on our great city's streets. Let us call her The New Woman. She is smart and sophisticated, with an air of independence about her, and so casual about her looks, clothes, and manners as to be almost slapdash—in a wildly stylish fashion. She, we are certain, represents the wave of the future. We share her restlessness. We understand her determination to free herself from the shackles of the Great War's era and discover what life is really all about.

zurich café: version two

One evening in 1916 at the Cabaret Voltaire, Hugo Ball picking up the French-German dictionary lying on the table next to his beer, opening it, and stabbing a random page with his letter opener.

The word the letter opener chooses is French babytalk for *hobbyhorse*.

In Romanian et cetera.

the painter

You giving anything to marry Raoul. All he had to do was agree to leave his wife. Your relationship with him would have thrived, had he not regularly disparaged your desire to wed, calling it *your bourgeois inclination*. Had he not repeatedly proposed you might spend your time more productively sniffing out a better job to support him so he could get on with cleansing Germany's calcified society.

His behavior prompted you in 1920 to write the short story "The Painter," whose one-and-a-half-page narrative involves an artist who is thrown into spiritual crisis when his wife asks him to do the dishes.

three phrases from hugo ball's manifesto
1. Fog paroxysm.
2. A cat meows.
3. Dada m'dada dada mhm,
   dada deradada, dada Hue, dada Tza.

hans richter reminisces about hannah höch's contribution to dada
Her input was extraordinarily beneficial to everyone—her ability to conjure up sandwiches, beer, and coffee for us despite the shortage of money was remarkable.

zurich café: version three
One evening in 1916 at the et cetera,
Richard Huelsenbeck et cetera.
       Et cetera.

wish image : c.
André Breton, one year before Hannah Höch steps into the crowded gallery on the arm of its owner: *Dada, very fortunately, is no longer an issue and its funeral, about May 1921, caused no rioting. Let there be Surrealism.*

wish image : d.

I thought the war would never end, George Grosz telling an interviewer in May 1959, two months before he drinks too much and jumbles down a flight of stairs into his limitations. *And perhaps it never did.*

kurt schwitters reminisces about hannah höch's contribution to dada

We all live twenty-four minutes too late, don't we?

three phrases from richard huelsenbeck's manifesto

1. A pig squeals in Butcher Nuttke's cellar.
2. To sit in a chair for a single moment is to risk one's life.
3.

art history textbook, revised edition

George Grosz and John Heartfield took against Höch's work almost immediately and aimed to have it excluded from the First International Dada Fair. Held between 30 June and 25 August 1920, the Berlin show subverted the traditional academic art exhibition by cramming the walls, ceiling, and floor of the small Galerie Otto Burchard on Lützowuferstraße with 174 posters, photomontages, and assemblages. Despite charging a considerable admission fee— three marks thirty, higher than the one cited in the catalogue—the enterprise proved a commercial failure. Höch was allowed to participate only when Hausmann threatened to withdraw his own work if hers was barred.

Most of what she exhibited has been lost, but her large-scale pho-tomontage, Cut with the Kitchen Knife Through the Last Weimar Beer-Belly Cultural Epoch in Germany—*a forceful commentary on gender roles in the postwar years composed of a teeming array of texts and images convulsed across the canvas (Höch clipped and rear-ranged bits from product catalogues, printed broadsides, magazines, journals, and newspapers into her vast kaleidoscopic composition, then added watercolor highlights)—ironically turned out to be one of the most prominently displayed and well-received works of the show.*

A photograph of Höch cradling one of her curious Dada dolls at the opening reveals her sporting an astonishing science-fiction getup. That notwithstanding, she never relished the exhibitionist element of the movement. Rather, she was embarrassed by the bohemian antics of her male confederates—even if she often found herself appearing in supporting roles.

the manifesto hannah höch never wrote
Your belief in reason and progress did this, got us to this point, your bourgeois meta-physics, and we are here to end it.

My work on women's magazines woke me to the difference between media and reality. It provided me as well with the raw material for my project. I wanted to collect everything that seemed of value or might eventually be needed. I wanted to eat boundaries. I wanted to depict brides as the mannequins, machines, and children they are.

The grammar of art, I wanted to prove, is doubt.

204

i spoke to her as a woman, but she answered me as a man

Seven years after meeting Raoul Hausmann, you leaving him. Without a final conversation. Without a goodbye. You not being there anymore those last few months.

Although you are the one who brings about the split, the following year will prove the most depleted of your life—bewildering, multilayered, jumpy, unspeakably lonely. You looking inside yourself and finding only grief. Around your friends you pretending everything is all right. They pretending everything is all right back, believing that must be what you want.

It taking nearly four years to retrieve yourself from yourself. When you do, you coming upon Mathilda Brugman walking beside you—Til—who likes to dress up as a man in a dark suit and tie, talk linguistics, and write poetry based on sound, rhythm, and page design rather than meaning.

You moving to The Hague to be with her.

You moving back to Berlin as a couple.

Your story a long happy ending until Til leaves you without a final goodbye. It hitting you after the fact that she hasn't been with you those last few months.

Your whole life, you coming to fathom, having been a science of imaginary solutions.

And so you marrying a traveling salesman twenty-two years younger than you, a convicted pedophile who likes to expose himself and jerk off in front of little girls in schoolyards, a man whom the German government will castrate shortly before your wedding in accordance with the law.

You marrying Kurt Matthies, aware before your second date that you will divorce him within half a dozen years—never predicting Kurt will in fact leave you first for one of your closest girlfriends.

wish image : e.

Fundamentally, André Breton telling an interviewer in July 1966, two months before he drifts off quietly among the readymades in his dreams, *since Dada we have done nothing.*

this dark fruit : does anyone hear me burning?

when I was still alive   when I was still alive   when I was still alive
before the pistol   before the pistol   before the pistol

barrel on tongue   barrel the tongue   barrel on tongue

when the trigger—   when the trigger —   when the trigger —

how odd   how odd   how odd

terrible colorless silence
when the —

just little Rudi rapping
at the door behind me

mommy mommy let me

and me kneeling by the
bed elbows on mattress

praying to the muzzle

terrible colorless silence
when the —

just little Rudi rapping
at the door behind me

mommy mommy let me

and me kneeling by the
bed elbows on mattress

praying to the muzzle

terrible colorless silence
when the —

just little Rudi rapping
at the door behind me

*mommy **mommy** let me*

and **me** kneeling by the
bed elbows on **mattress**

praying to the muzzle

Robert always telling
me *stop it Magda stop
talking nonsense*

you have no —

you're scaring the child

of course I am

the autistics constantly
planting things in my
mouth

Robert always telling
me *stop it Magda **stop**
talking nonsense*

you have no —

you're scaring the child

of course I am

the autistics constantly
planting things in my
mouth

Robert always telling
me *stop it Magda stop
talking nonsense*

you have no **no** *—*

you're scaring the child

of course I am

the autistics constantly
planting things **in my
mouth**

bullet ideas	bullet ideas	bullet ideas
poems	poems	poems
terrible colorless silence and next sparkly islands of activity	terrible colorless silence and next sparkly islands of activity	terrible colorless silence and next sparkly islands of activity
this unending second	this unending second	this unending second
trigger prayers	trigger prayers	trigger prayers

me telling him telling
Robert *I can' t bear the*
idea of cremation

me telling him telling
Robert *I can' t bear the*
idea of cremation

me telling him telling
Robert *I can' t bear the*
idea of cremation

bury the thing of me
that's left ... **please**

bury the thing of me
that's left ... please

bury the thing of me
that's left ... **please**

make me a Christian
god-damn it

make me a Christian
god-damn it

make me a Christian
god-damn it

laughing over Riesling:
you really must outgrow
your evolutionary retar-
dation my love

laughing over Riesling:
you really must outgrow
your evolutionary retar-
dation my love

laughing over Riesling:
you really must outgrow
your evolutionary retar-
dation my **love**

— is what he —

— is what he —

— is what he —

member in good stand-
ing of the German Free-
thinkers League

member in good stand-
ing of the German Free-
thinkers League

member in good stand-
ing of the German Free-
thinkers League

*how can you believe in
God if not in Mother
Goose?*

*how can you believe in
God if not in Mother
Goose?*

*how can you **believe** in
God if not in Mother
Goose?*

*and not a single word
in the Gospel praising
intelligence —*

*and not a single word
in the Gospel praising
intelligence —*

*and not a single word
in the **Gospel** praising
intelligence —*

and next that terrible
colorless silence and —

and next that **terrible**
colorless silence and —

and next that terrible
colorless silence and —

does anyone hear me
burning?

does anyone hear me
burning?

does anyone hear me
burning?

Magda Müller is in
flames

the belly of Berlin's first
crematorium

built above the shrieks
of   Wedding's   first
graveyard

they call it *an improve-
ment* —

progressive approach to

Magda Müller is in
flames

the belly of Berlin's first
crematorium

built above the shrieks
of   Wedding's   first
graveyard

they call it *an improve-
ment* —

progressive approach to

Magda Müller is **in**
flames

the belly of Berlin's first
crematorium

built above the **shrieks**
of   Wedding's   first
graveyard

they **call** it *an improve-
ment* —

progressive approach to

but this is what I know   but this is what I know   but this is what I know

Magda Müller's skin is flaking into ashes   Magda Müller's skin is flaking into ashes   Magda Müller's skin is flaking into ashes

each wing of this octagon packed with a thousand urns   each wing of this octagon packed with a thousand urns   each wing of this octagon packed with a thousand urns

his growing sense of replenishment   his growing sense of replenishment   his growing sense of replenishment

factories rumbling over the walls   factories rumbling over the walls   factories rumbling over the walls

workshops banging across Gerichtstraße   workshops banging across Gerichtstraße   workshops banging across Gerichtstraße what will come of this?   what will come of this?   what will come of **this**?

Robert sitting above me   Robert sitting above me   Robert sitting above me
on a bench in the mourn-   on a bench in the **mourn-**   on a bench in the mourn-
ing hall contemplating   ing hall contemplating   ing hall contemplating
the huge snake sunk into   the huge snake sunk into   the huge snake sunk **into**
the terrazzo floor   the terrazzo floor   the terrazzo floor

I can feel his relief   I can feel his **relief**   I can feel his relief

because crazy Magda is   because crazy Magda is   **because** crazy Magda is
finally on fire   finally on fire   finally on fire

sorry for the pain she   sorry for the pain she   sorry for the pain she
caused him because she   caused him because **she**   caused him because she
wasn't him   wasn't him   wasn't him

caused Rudi because she   caused Rudi because she   caused Rudi because **she**
came to think of him by the came to think of him by   came to think of him by
time he was three as a scar the time he was three as   the time he **was** three as
that—   a scar that —   a scar that —

mouths chattering away   mouths chattering away   mouths chattering away
inside her mouth   inside **her** mouth   inside her **mouth**

for wanting change   for wanting change   for wanting change

for not wanting change   for not **wanting** change   for not wanting change

for wanting time to run   for wanting time to run   for **wanting** time to run
out   out   out

for wanting more of it   for **wanting** more of it   for wanting more of it

for not noticing the
— what?

for not noticing the
— what?

for not noticing the
— what?

pulped lemon brighten-
ing the edge of winter
sky

pulped lemon brighten-
ing the edge of winter
sky

pulped lemon brighten-
ing the edge of winter
sky

flesh creped over the
back of his hand

flesh creped over the
back of his hand

flesh creped over the
back of his hand

ghosts winding up being
the parts of life you never
finished

ghosts winding up being
the parts of life you never
finished

ghosts winding up being
the parts of life you never
finished

for not taking time to
touch more things

for not taking time to
touch more things

for not taking time to
touch more things

my red heaven

the flesh creped over the   the flesh creped over the   the flesh creped over the

back of his —   back of his —   back of his —

against my cheek   against my cheek   against my cheek

delicate entanglement —   delicate entanglement —   delicate entanglement —

apologizing too much   apologizing too much   apologizing too much

never enough   never enough   never enough

even when she knew it
wou —

even when she knew it
wou —

even when she knew it
wou —

how we ate plums and
drank Riesling all after-
noon by the lake

how we ate plums and
drank Riesling all after-
noon by the lake

how we ate plums and
drank Riesling all after-
noon by the lake

cattail banks

cattail banks

cattail banks

Magda hate-loving him

Magda hate-loving him

Magda hate-loving him

despising herself for it

despising herself for it

despising herself for it

biting down on this
warm juicy dark fruit
between her fingers

biting down on this
warm juicy dark fruit
between her fingers

biting down on this
warm juicy dark fruit
between her fingers

time streaking in from
both directions at once

time streaking in from
both directions at once

time streaking in from
both directions at once

no matter what we did

no matter what we did

no matter what we did

never forgiving him for
my life — his life

never forgiving him for
my life —— his life

never forgiving him for
my life —— his life

never for that

never for that

never for that

for this

for this

for this

for the —

for the —

for the —

the —

the —

the —

café elektric : we have come loose from ourselves

—freakish thing isn't that we die, is it, realizes the technician as he screws down
the gas jets in Magda Müller's oven, *but
that anyone is still left alive.*

Gustav Ucicky (who will claim throughout his
life—without offering any proof—that he is the
illegitimate son of Gustav Klimt) calls it a wrap on
Marlene Dietrich's last scene in *Café Elektric*, the
movie he has been shooting six hundred and fifty
kilometers to the southeast, and Marlene, reaching
up automatically to fuss with her hair, lets in this
half-thought: *Son of a bitch what I would give for a
whiskey.*

Hannah Arendt and Martin Heidegger step arm in arm through the main doors of the Arnhold Villa into the salon's fuss, where they catch a glimpse, above the heads of the other guests, of the scarlet traces threading the sky over Lake Wannsee through the large windows on the far end of the room. Hannah instinctively presses Martin's arm tighter.

Down the block a train bedlams through the Wannsee Station on its way into the city. Johann Pfeiffer, en route to enroll at the university, shuts *Passionate Journey*, Frans Masereel's wordless novel in woodcuts, and looks out the window the very instant Berlin's trashed backsides start rushing past.

Across from him sits the no-longer-thin, no-longer-hirsute Walter Gropius, making notes for the party he will throw upon his return to Weimar next week. Whenever the regularly smoldering tensions among his Bauhaus faculty spark into conflagration, Walter always throws a party. In his leather-bound journal, he writes: *2 naked women / 1 naked man = painted silver to slither. Eerie music / flashing lights. Silver paper to cover walls + large chute from ground floor to basement to end in—rubber mats? pillow mountain? Many white pellets to be thrown.*

Beside Walter Gropius sits his second wife, Ise, endeavoring to doze, yet returning repeatedly to Walter's first wife, Alma, meaty-eared, razor-lipped, eyes marginally uncoordinated, whom she has successfully not thought about for nearly seven months, and to how that bitch eats men like bonbons, slipping from Gustav Klimt's arms into Gustav Mahler's, Gustav Mahler's into Oskar Kokoschka's, Oskar Kokoschka's into Waltchen's, Waltchen's into Franz Werfel's. *She seems to have confused trying every*thing *once,* Ise reasons, *with trying every*one *once.* A smile flourishes on her face at the turn of phrase.

Ise doesn't notice out the window a young woman, Anna Handke, gently lay her infant down in the middle of the street and depart. Anna will refuse to pick it up again, telling the two policemen who materialize she can no longer figure out how to feed it.

[[a radiant system]]

The conductor in rimless glasses bends down to ask the dozing woman in the fascinator with black birdcage veil for her ticket, asking himself: *What kind of sandwich has Hilde made me this evening—cheese—or salami—or—I hope it's eggs. Eggs would be a nice bit of change.*

In the midst of locking up her asparagus stall for the night, squat red-faced Elli Schulz pauses to watch the train bedlam past and stretches her throbby back. *A minute*, she tells herself, *a minute, and it will be good as new.*

Max Liebermann, the eighty-year-old Impressionist painter, scrooches down in the back row of the packed Marmorhaus theater, glaring at the newsreels before the feature begins, sorely aware this is what the last pterodactyl must have felt like—forlorn, hopelessly out of step with its time, dead in some absolute sense years before the reaper actually visits. *I think I've heard of Max Liebermann—I wonder who he was*, people in fifty years, Max knows, won't ever say.

Milosh Fazenta, switchblade in his back pocket, smiles ob-
sequiously at the bull-chested Prussian cop passing in the
opposite direction on the street. (One afternoon sixteen years
from now three SS guards for fun will use the cop's pink
downward-pointing triangle as target practice at an estab-
lishment in southeastern Poland few people will have heard
about.) The cop nods back, vacant-faced as a card shark,
thinking to himself: *Gypsy shit.*

Bruno Metzger closes his eyes, pinches
off his nostrils, and slips below the
pool's surface in the Friedrichstraße
public baths, drifting underwater like
a content walrus, reveling in his giddy
weightlessness, how the tiled walls and
human voices cut off, how beneath the
water sound slows, congests, closes in
until the entire world becomes no more
than Bruno Metzger, who observes
himself open his butcher shop tomorrow morning, the spotless pleasure of
bringing down his cleaver through the
day's first hog hock.

[[bounding for birds]]

—and did Olga tell me to buy a bag of flour or was it sugar? Berthold Schwarz asks himself, coming up short as he pushes against the corner grocery's door, only to learn it is already locked for the day, although he can still make out dim shapes moving inside—

—as, in town from Paris to visit Hannah Höch's new exhibition and catch up with old friends, Otto Freundlich steps off the U-Bahn into the ruckus of the Kurfürstenstraße platform. The idea for his next painting gyres in. Its title, he comprehends without warning, will be *My Red Heaven*, and it will consist of an abstract flurry of quadrilateral shapes forging three color strata down a large canvas: reds at the top; grays, greens, whites, and blues in the middle; blacks at the bottom. Otto doesn't know it will take another half decade before he can plunge in. Other ambitions will broil into his life first, including the vision for what he believes (although this isn't the case) to be his masterwork: a highway lined with non-figurative sculptures stretching from Paris to Moscow that shows what peace and brotherhood could look like. A decade, and another work of his will be featured on the cover of the catalogue for The Degenerate Art Exhibition staged in Munich. A sculpture called *The New Man*, it will stand nearly one and a half meters tall and resemble a modernist rendition of one of those stone heads on Easter Island. Four

years later it will disappear, as will most of Otto's
art, as will Otto himself. First, though, he will go
into hiding in the Pyrenees, be denounced and
arrested in Saint-Martin-de-Fenouillet, a tiny
mountain village about two hundred kilometers
southeast of Montpellier, having with a miscon-
strued sense of faith in reason written a personal
letter of protest to the highest local authorities
when told he must register as a Jew under the
Vichy regulations. On 9 March, 1943, sixty-four,
with achy feet and bum knee, Otto will hoist
himself up into train No. 907, which will babel
him to the Lublin-Majdanek extermination camp
in southeastern Poland, the first to be discovered
by the Soviet troops eighteen months later. The
last thing Otto will see before the cattle-car door
slams shut and bolts is a little buttery-blond boy
with slingshot launching a frail white paper glider
into the bluewhite dawn. Exhaustion, not Zyklon
B, will claim Otto before the sun sets on his first
day at his new home, yet now, walking up the
stairs from the U-Bahn onto the nattering street,
nothing exists in his head except one question:
Did I just take the wrong exit again?

Staring over at her flat's door, done waiting and never
done waiting for her diplomat, Marianne says aloud, both
to feel the words from inside and to hear them from outside: *My love is beating me up.*

The little buttery-blond boy trots down the staircase past Marianne's door and a fat lady ascending whose skirt and blouse are so tight it seems as if a girl has transformed into a woman within seconds (seven years from now the boy will notice his regular teachers begin mysteriously disappearing from his classrooms, one by one, replaced without comment by a sterner, grimmer, dimmer species altogether), the thought hitting him: *Potato dumplings…who's cooking potato dumplings?*—

—as the custodian stops sweeping the path in front of the panther cage at the zoo long enough to notice how tired the pacing animal's gaze has grown against the flickering bars. A line from that poem he was forced to memorize back in grammar school (he can't quite reassemble the author's name) eels up through him: *To him, there seem to be a thousand bars and back behind those thousand bars no world.* The custodian still hasn't figured out what that means. *If poets would just stop beating around the goddamn bush and—*

[[skin waving goodbye]]

—and Renate Engel rides the escalator from first to ground floor in KaDeWe, Europe's largest department store, seven floors, twenty-four thousand square meters, one of the last customers of the evening, savoring the bracing knowledge she doesn't look like ordinary women, but rather a representative from another, more glorious race. She secretly relishes her disconcertingly long legs, aquiline nose, high cheekbones, pearly bunned hair, dark-brick lipstick, assertive breasts, merciless black felt hat, shoulderless black dress, disabling poise, formidable self-possession. *How thankful I am*, Renate tells herself (as she conscientiously does several times every day in accordance with the Hindu-Nazi teachings she studies with Walther Wüst, the young doctor of philosophy down at the University of Munich, in a series of private monthly lessons), surveying the luxury goods as they rise to meet her, *life is so full, so magnificent, so rich with wonder and joy and energy and spirit, just like me.*

Standing at her kitchen table, aproned Adina Kleid takes in her husband, Chaim, and two boys, Amir and Alim, with affectionate pride tinctured with churning resentment as she leans forward to light the candles and welcome Shabbat into their home. *Baruch atah, Adonai, Eloheinu*, she commences, deciding this might be a good night to trim her toenails.

Perched at a waist-high table in the foyer of the Arnhold Villa, Magnus Hirschfeld sips Sekt and feasts on
the trio's rendition of *Sinfonia 1 C-Major* enlacing
itself before him—its arithmetical grace, its clarity, its
balance, its precision, its annihilating perfection—recalling with satisfaction Debussy's description of Bach
as the benevolent god to whom all composers should
offer a prayer in order to defend themselves against the
dissonance of mediocrity.

In the flat across the hall from Adina
Kleid's, deferential Stanisław and Ha-
lina Banaszynski sit stiffly at the foot
of Krystyna's—their fifteen-year-old
daughter's—bed, looking on while
the doctor searches the girl's wrist for
a pulse, but less and less, Krystyna's
shiny eyes slitted open, the muscles
in her face relaxed beyond life, her
mouth wide and startled by what
has pounced her fewer than five days
after that sickly man in the U-Bahn
sneezed, sharing with Krystyna
influenza's coughs, sweats, shaking
chills, and dry heaves, how if she had
stepped into a different car, or into
the same car through the other door,
or decided to walk rather than train
home from school, or stayed behind
with friends that afternoon to struggle
through a few more lines of Latin
in a nearby café, or been born on a

Thursday rather than a Monday, or turned her head away from that man a second earlier, or believed more firmly in God, or less firmly in the devil, or planned to be a nurse rather than a teacher, a teacher rather than a baker's assistant, something else might have come to pass, who could say what, a nice handsome soldier in a crisp uniform walking into her hopefulness, a simple happy marriage, a complicated unhappy one, an uneventful union where she never quite followed through with the plans she made, although she was always making them, one after another after another, yet it didn't matter because Krystyna came to believe everything occurred for a reason—except this storm that tore through her flat adolescence.

[[twenty-seven seconds ago]]

The last time I bought a painting for such a price it had two floating cows in it, one blue and one green, the beaky bald hunchbacked poet and cabaret critic Max Herrmann-Neisse declaims from the luxurious chair that looks as if it might be devouring him at George Grosz's dinner party. *That dolt's has only one earth-bound horse, and, arguably, it is loose-stool brown. To be honest, I'm not quite sure how one could possibly feel one is getting one's money's worth with such a tertiary faux pas.*

Between the beginning and the end of Max's observation, Otto Dix determines he will make his excuses to George and the others and return home to spill back into his studio's stillness and that painting about the battered, the consumed, the disemboweled emblem of this unusable country.

Odo Bergmann delivers the second fast fist to his girlfriend Zilli Keller's tummy in the kitchen of their flat across from Georg Grosz's, the evanescent grief swerving into him: *I really wish she didn't make me do this to her all the time.*

Robert Musil strolls cheerfully down a gravel path in the Tiergarten, light ashing everywhere, past a man in threadbare blazer sans tie propelling himself quickly in the opposite direction (a journalist? a young professor?), past a meadow circulating with baby prams, chuffing dogs, cuddling couples, and a late game of football. Robert was in town just a few months ago for Rilke's memorial service. Now he is here from Vienna six days to continue research on his novel-in-progress, tentatively titled *The Man Without Qualities*, which he has been buffeting against for six years, and whose end—a point of light no bigger than a match specking the midnight horizon—he has seriously started worrying may never draw nearer. The more he pens, the more characters and ideas surge up around him and it all gets unconscionably out of control, like the simple act of beheading a chicken sometimes can. Robert has never made a steady income, has thrown his family into financial crisis more than once...yet right now he believes more than anything (taking a deep breath of candied night air flowing into the city from the west) it isn't we who do the thinking. It is life that does the thinking all around us. Let life think. Let morality be a profusion of life's possibilities.

[[the heat of our thoughts]]

On his balcony with a hand-sized view of the Tiergarten's tree-tops, a tram driver leans back in his wooden chair, feet propped on the banister, arranging comfort and a cigarette, illumination pervading him: *One regret I am determined not to have on my deathbed, Silvia, is that I didn't kiss you enough.*

Inside the radio station near Gendarmen-markt, the session musicians strike up. Minna Brandt clasps her hands before her as if in prayer while picturing the thousands of people across the capital awaiting the arrival of her voice with anticipation. Her pulse spurs. Her lips part. She leans toward the microphone, lifting her eyes to the ceiling for inspiration, and sings: *Abandoned, abandoned, abandoned am I like a stone upon the road—*

The young man in the threadbare blazer sans tie propelling himself past Robert Musil in the opposite direction is Ludwig Wittgenstein, thirty eight, degreeless, fuddled with three beers, on his way to Weimar tomorrow to compile more ideas for designing his sister Margaret's austere house back in overwrought Vienna. There will be no baseboards in it. There will be nothing but bare bulbs. It will take him a full year to devise the door handles, another the radiators. Nearly finished, Ludwig will demand the entire ceiling be raised thirty millimeters. It is impossible to determine if he ever mulls over the fact that three of his five brothers—Hans, the musical prodigy; Kurt, the military officer during the war; Rudi, the promising chemistry student attending university here—committed suicide. Yet it is clear he isn't mulling it over at present, Hans drowning himself in the Chesapeake Bay on a pilgrimage to lose himself in America; Kurt blowing out his brains when the Austrian troops he commanded refused to obey his orders and deserted en masse; Rudi asking the pianist at the corner bar to play that gushy folksong, "Abandoned, Abandoned, Abandoned Am I," before ordering a glass of milk, mixing in a tiny vial of potassium cyanide, and chugging down the brew in front of the regulars. Rather, this failed gardener and primary school teacher who gave away his family fortune almost a decade ago, furnishes his rooms with deck chairs, and bolts plate after plate of cream doughnuts while watching his favorite movies, is trolling for the rough-trade boys who sell themselves in the bushy corner of the park nearest the Reichstag, shame and fury searing through his veins, pondering: *If I interpret my thought as one of Mussolini's, and God sees it as one of Buster Keaton's, who is right?*

By the way, whatever became of that bright lad Nikolas? Martin Heidegger asks Arnold Schoenberg about their mutual academic acquaintance, his shoulder brushing against Emil Jannings' behind him. Arnold Schoenberg answers flatly: History.

On the eve of her twenty-fifth birthday (she will treat herself and three of her closest girlfriends to a round of beer, Königsberger Klopse, and boiled potatoes at the local Ratskeller tomorrow evening by way of celebration), elfin Brigitte Hoffmann receives another light cape from another patron over the cloakroom counter in the lobby of the Metropol Theater (a well-dressed gentleman not much older than she, sporting that tidily cropped gray hair and fastidiously contained mien of The German Professional) minutes before the curtain goes up on tonight's operetta (Franz Lehár's *Count of Luxembourg*, that cute one about an impoverished aristocrat and glamorous opera singer who enter into a sham marriage without ever meeting each other, only to fall in love at first sight later, unaware they are already husband and wife), and this intuition ripples into her heart and out again: *The truth is every one of the two billion people on this planet is bored beyond imagining. I'm bored. He's bored. The people over there filing into the theater. We're just trying to distract ourselves from each other a little while any lousy-stupid way we—*

Listen, Emil, you know as well as I that time is Christianity's fault, Max Sievers, chairman of the German Freethinkers League, explains to the actor, his shoulder brushing against Schoenberg's behind him. Max and Emil stand side by side, attending the pale creamy glow and scarlet streaks above the lake. *Everything worked perfectly before the mackerel snappers belly-ached onto the scene. Every second circulated inside every other. Yesterday and tomorrow lived inside every Now. And then, poof, our culture conjured up the quite bizarre notion that we possess bags full of sin we are obliged to drag around behind us, an enchanted nowhere it is our duty to reach, a timetable existence that will somehow lead us to some dull, endless séance privée—which capitalism, mind you, has been only too happy to soak up and propagate for its own profitable ends. What a crock of goatshit. How on earth did humanity ever allow itself to be bamboozled so badly?*

Emil cracks up in pantomime, performing levity instead of living it, although he isn't really listening to anything Max is saying.

[[a chair is a very difficult object]]

—as, softening into sleep, Sonya, Käthe Kollwitz's live-in housekeeper, orchestrates tomorrow's to-do list: 1. buy flowers; 2. Apfelkuchen;
3. sharpen knives; 4. look up *numinous*; 5. sharpen knives; 6. continue to hope for more; 7. dust living room; 8. no good deed ever goes
unpunished; 9. dust—; 10. wish—; 11. dust—; 12. —

—as Hannah Höch circulates through the teeming gallery
lined with her work, smiling, shaking hands, clinking glasses,
making small talk, wishing at this bend in her career she could
be more excited by the flap going on around her, the accident
of evenings like this, how with the arrival of such middling rec-
ognition she can sense herself with each in-suck of air becoming more stupid and strident and mercilessly, sanctimoniously
inflexible.

The author suffering from a bad case of heartburn
(that peppery turnip stew never agrees with him even
though he keeps returning to the café around the corner that serves it because it is cheap and filling and
could no doubt be much worse) sits at his desk overlooking Helmholtzplatz, listening to the couple going
at it in the flat above, and pencils: *The Doberman's
name is Delia. Delia won't see the end of this day. She
doesn't know that. What she knows is she's on the longest,
most glorious walk of her life.*

Four meters above the author's head, Egon Lehmann works his way down Kristel Weber's naked astonishment with his tongue—from boy breasts, to soft tummy, to indented belly button, where he lingers as—

—as Alfred Phillips stands among throngs of the dead gathered on the Adlon's rooftop, watching the immense flaming ocean gather over the capital, murmuring in unison with the others who have shed their bodies, sexes, injuries, illnesses: *We have come loose from ourselves. The animals are leaving. Our children, our spouses, our friends, our colleagues, our brothers, our sisters, our mothers, our fathers are busy putting us behind them. All that remains is our bungled joy, the sensation of those moments we've forgotten that were important only as they were passing ...*

[[a hundred different movies]]

Oskar Kokoschka prefers the Münzis, the heavily pregnant tarts that hover in the hazy lamp halos. They're expensive, yes, but those hard rotund bellies, the way they. Good omens for his work. Like the fire that broke out in Pöchlarn days after he was born. Spirit announcement. Advent of. Mostly because he can't stop loving Alma, who left him for that asshole architect who isn't the next anybody. That's why he built the gynoid doll of her. That's why he prayed to it daily. Only it didn't help and so he smashed it against the back of the sofa in the middle of George Grosz's party in front of all his. Except now there is this creeping horror of the nine-year-old's tiny proficient fingers stroking his upper thigh as her busted-toothed mother, cutting scars up and down her right arm, covers his face with hot wet sucking kisses and Oskar pulls away and throws himself deeper into the haloed night.

If I may be so bold, Hannah Arendt explains in the bit-by-bit warmer and more humid lobby to Walter Benjamin (without having caught his name), *I don't believe you fully understand my position. What I mean to say is there will always be rebels. And you know who they are: the mutinous poets, painters, sculptors, musicians, dancers, mystics, thinkers, journalists like yourself, and other outcasts willing to accept personal sacrifice in the name of principle. They live in the shadows. They're poor. The state has little tolerance for them. Mass propaganda has conditioned society to belittle them as parasites and traitors. They live that way, not because it's exotic or adventurous, but because to collaborate with radical evil is to betray all that is beautiful and good.*

Walter Benjamin shakes his head
thoughtfully, as if absorbing all Hannah has to say, weighing it carefully,
thinking to himself: *Nice breasts.*

The boxer delivers the second fast fist to his opponent's stunned
face in the makeshift ring behind the train factory in which he
just completed a nine-hour shift, an evanescent grief swerving
into him: *I really wish he didn't make me do this to him.*

Günter Graf genuflects on his achy knees in the Potsdammer Platz
intersection, blowtorch in hand, trying with his team to finish
repairs to the tracks before dawn. Glancing up, it occurs to him
the streets around here are even busier at night than during the
day, with pleasure seekers, motorcars, horse-drawn garbage carts,
and those damn bicycles weaving in and out. A tram rolls by on
the opposite tracks, gas lamps shivering across its windows. *Can't
crap money like them can,* Günter tells himself, flipping down his
visor and getting back to work. *Wish I could, 'cept the harder a man
works, the more Jesus fucking hates him.*

I thought Minna Brandt had suffered some sort of tragic death, the cellist
Arno Vogt explains during his break to one of the Arnhold daughters. (He
can't tell which.) *Oh, heavens no,* Anna-Maria replies gaily, *that was just
her career.*

Adolf Hitler pops another chocolate-covered marzipan square onto his tongue as his plane taxis toward the runway. He is busy behind his forehead reliving this morning's event with his supporters and the press, savoring how easily he handled those pain-in-the-ass journalists with a combination of force, obfuscation, and strategic deception. Engines revving, Adolf senses his eyes beginning to close, his consciousness beginning to unbuckle. A few seconds later, he is reliving nothing at all.

[[the noise knowledge makes]]

On the thin single mattress in a corner of the unpainted tenement room two blocks away from Kurfürstenstraße, Emilie the transvestite secretly grits her teeth and swallows Billie Wilder's cum, neither gratified nor aroused by Billie's caught breaths, learning with a shock, as if for the first time, the kike's load tastes like vinegar and dead feet.

On the sidewalk below, Carl Fischer and an Amazon (Hilda Huber, the third of the buttery-blond boy's teachers—his favorite, always ready with a smile, a supportive remark, a gentle hand upon his shoulder—to drop out of his universe seven years from today) are interrupted by the first fireworks of the evening bursting above them in a rain of golden hair threads and green stars.

A gleeful murmuration rising from the crowds.

Three seats back from Adolf Hitler, Erich Maria Berger, one of Joseph Goebbels' staff, has just closed his eyes as well—not to doze, but rather to admire the Gauleiter ever more thoroughly. Erich never fails to be impressed by how savvy Goebbels is, how many planetary systems can inhabit such an intelligence at once. Ten days ago Erich accompanied him to a graveyard to speak at the funeral for a Brownshirt beaten and knifed during a street skirmish with the Communists in Wedding.

On the drive there, Goebbels talked nonstop about various typographical changes he wanted made to his newspaper, *Der Angriff,* whose first issue appears next week. Even as he walked past the paramilitaries lining the path to the grave, Goebbels continued issuing instructions to Erich under his breath. Yet at the site itself something converged inside him. He scowled at his boots, looked up at the small crowd gathered before him, stations switched behind his eyes, and he launched into a heart-hammering oration about the heroism of the murdered man. Goebbels vowed vengeance. Vowed revolution. Vowed an end to oppression by the exploiters and rejuvenation of the Germanic nations. You could feel the bystanders spark with outrage and purpose. Back in the car, he turned to Erich and asked, scratching his cheek: *Remind me again, Herr Berger—what was that dead chap's name?* Erich told him. *Excellent,* the Gauleiter replied. *Echt German. May I ask you your thoughts on Grobe Deutschmeister? It feels quite a manly font to me. Does it feel quite manly to you?—*

—as a greasy-faced pimp in black lipstick, black eyeliner, and white makeup replaces the Amazon. Laying a bird-bones hand upon Carl's shoulder, he says in a gelatinous French accent: *A male goose whose neck you cut at just the right ecstatic instant will give you the most delicious frisson, monsieur. Think about it—the ravishments of sodomy, bestiality, faggotry, necrophilia, and sadism all in one beatific flash! What about it?* Carl shakes off the man's hand in disgust, dodges around him, on the spot abandoning tonight's project. The pimp calls after him as Carl hustles down the street: *Gastronomy, too, monsieur! You can eat the bird when you're done! We'll cook him up for you! Imagine, monsieur! Heaven on earth!*

[[mother eating her own uterus]]

The boy with the grimy face who saw what the beer truck did to that man snuggles beneath a sheet atop the chunky straw mattress with his three brothers angling for position, settling with satisfaction on an insight that has been trying to invent itself in him all day: *Once we die we all become the same age.*

Clocks are for the young, the legless gypsy woman realizes, waiting for her son to pick her up off the curb and wheel her home behind him in his wooden wagon—*for those who lack soul and wings, but I have finally grown old enough to move freely through time—*

Albert Einstein farts demurely while practicing his violin, thinks *I believe that was a B-flat,* stops, cups the bitter aroma in his palm and brings it up to his nose, as—

—as Werner Heisenberg capsizes into sleep in a Leipzig hotel his last thought landing *that wasn't such a bad talk … nothing great but certainly passable* as Vladimir Nabokov peers out the black train window scudding through the Czechoslovakian countryside to encounter only his own pasty reflection peering back as the German Shakespeare Club in Bochum closes out its week with *King Henry VIII* as in the midst of a late dinner with friends Mies van der Rohe all at once remembers that poor fellow his cab slid by this morning his face what had become of and shudders while slipping another forkful of asparagus between his lips as the little girl to whom Kafka once wrote letters about her doll's lovely holiday on a sunny Greek island bobs in a dreamless sleep, fingertips twitching, the last of Franz's magic words fading from her memory for good—

—as the pickpockets Lisa and Ursula close in on their final victim of the night (Kurt Severing, sensing the electrostatic currents streaming around him, out for a celebratory stroll across Alexanderplatz after dropping off his review at the newspaper office) as nearly seven hundred kilometers southeast his mother kisses Ernst Herbeck on the forehead and it visits him in his dream *a song is a kind of shared redness* as Alfred Brinkmann of Kiel becomes the latest star in the European chess firmament winning over grand-masters Bogoljubov and Nimzowitsch as elderly Julius the retired concierge sitting in the rocking chair interrupts elderly Anton the retired sommelier lying on the couch to ask *is there anything I can get for you before I wash up for bed love?* and Anton replying *everything and nothing my dear everything and nothing*—

—as Marlene Dietrich laughs in her sleep so loudly she wakes herself as Alban Berg wonders about the philosophical potential of the A-sharp as Bertolt Brecht watches his own dark piss foam in the flickery gas-lamp light and reek of

the octagonal pissoir at the edge
of Gendarmenmarkt following
an insipid performance of *Faust*
at the Prussian State Theater it
coming to him out of nowhere
of course Elizabeth is right I'll do
a German version of Gay's Beggar's
Opera *a musical I'll ask Weill to-*
morrow tell Aufricht I translated
the thing—

[[we have come loose from ourselves]]

—as Heinz Buchholz, the beer truck driver, eyes closed (heedless in seventeen years he will serve as the stenographer at the conference table in the Wolf's Lair one hot July day when the bomb hidden inside a briefcase at the far end blossoms into light and anarchy), dances a slow dance with his wife, Amanda, among white balloons and glittery reflecting balls at Bühlers Ballhaus, side by side with a pale redheaded girl with swan's neck in the arms of a tall thin wide-shouldered boy, doing no more than saying thank you for the warm press of Amanda's body, for this evening's spectacular sunset, for the fireworks beginning to quicken the sky as they entered, thank you even though he knows there's nobody to hear the words, because it doesn't matter, believing these minutes should last and last and last, even though they won't.

One of the passengers briefly comes awake as the plane banks, gaining altitude. He squints down, gratified, at Berlin receding below, canals and boulevards and housing blocks blackening into forests and lakes, and reaches over to pat his comrade on the wrist. Don't worry, Joseph, he says. Don't worry at all. I can feel it. Everything's going to be all—

squints down, gratified, at Berlin receding below, canals and
boulevards and housing blocks blackening into forests and lakes,
and reaches over to pat his comrade on the wrist. *Don't worry,
Joseph,* he says. *Don't worry at all. I can feel it. Everything's going
to be all —*

squints down, gratified, at Berlin receding below, canals and
boulevards and housing blocks blackening into forests and lakes,
and reaches over to pat his comrade on the wrist. *Don't worry,
Joseph,* he says. *Don't worry at all. I can feel it. Everything's going
to be all —*

squints down, gratified, at Berlin receding below, canals and
boulevards and housing blocks blackening into forests and lakes,
and reaches over to pat his comrade on the wrist. *Don't worry,
Joseph,* he says. *Don't worry at all. I can feel it. Everything's going
to be all —*

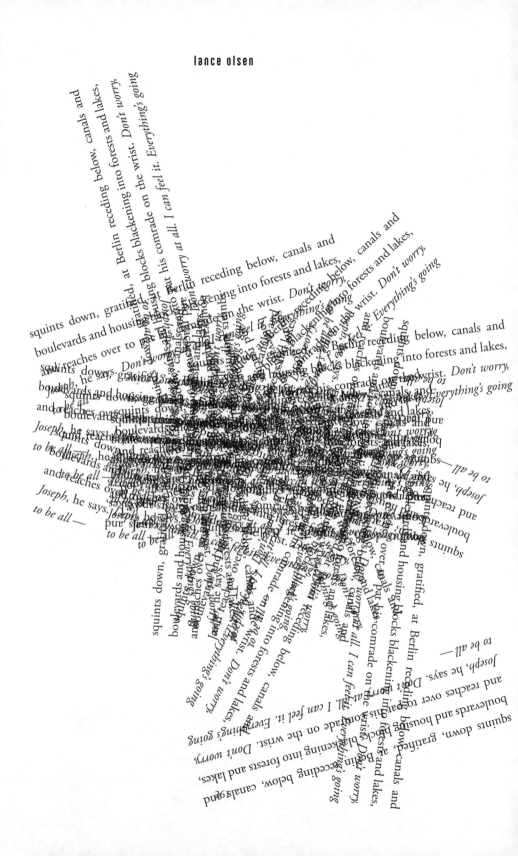

gaining

, canals

d lakes,

seph, he

-